FRANKENSTEIN

Abridged from Mary Shelley's famous story

illustrated by
TOM BARLING

today press

GROSSET & DUNLAP
A Filmways Company
Publishers · New York

First published 1976
by Grosset & Dunlap Inc. Publishers
New York

Copyright illustrations © Tom Barling 1976
Copyright text © Trewin Copplestone Publishing Ltd 1976
Originated and produced by
Trewin Copplestone Publishing Ltd

All rights reserved. No part of this publication
may be reproduced, recorded or transmitted in
any form or by any means, whether electronic or
mechanical, including photocopy, microfilm,
recording or any information storage and
retrieval system, without permission in writing
from Trewin Copplestone Publishing Ltd, London

Filmsetting by Photoprint Plates Ltd
Rayleigh, Essex
Originated and
Printed in Italy by
New Interlitho SpA, Milan

Library of Congress catalog card number 76-10060
ISBN: 0-448-12638-9

CHAPTER ONE

Robert Walton's Letters

To Mrs Saville, England
St Petersburgh, 11th December 1787

YOU will be pleased to hear that no disaster has accompanied my enterprise so far, despite your evil forebodings. I arrived here yesterday and as I walked in the streets of Petersburgh, the cold northern breeze playing upon my face filled me with delight because it had travelled from the regions to which I will be going. I am sure that the North Pole is not as desolate as people say for, in my imagination, I see it as a region of beauty and delight where the sun can always be seen. You must admit, dear Margaret, that I shall confer an inestimable benefit on mankind by discovering a new passage to those countries which, at present, can only be reached by a voyage of many months. In the six years since I decided to undertake this expedition I have hardened my body so that I could endure the cold. I accompanied whale-fishers on voyages in the North Sea and voluntarily endured cold, famine, thirst, and want of sleep.

This is the most favourable period for travelling in Russia, flying quickly over the snow in sledges; the cold is not excessive if you are wrapped in furs. I shall depart for Archangel in a fortnight and hire a ship, engaging as many sailors as I think necessary from those who are accustomed to the conditions. If I succeed, many months, perhaps years, will pass before you see me again. If I fail, you will see me again soon—or never.
    Your affectionate brother, Robert Walton.

To Mrs Saville, England
Archangel, 28th March 1788

I have hired a vessel and begun to engage sailors who appear to be dependable and courageous. But there is one need which I have not been able to satisfy: I have no friend, Margaret. When I am glowing with success or when I am assailed by disappointment there will be no-one to share my emotions. I have no-one near me who has a cultivated and capacious mind with tastes like my own, to approve or amend my plans. How such a friend would repair the faults of your poor brother! I shall certainly find no such friend among merchants and seamen. Yet some have feelings which rise above the roughness of their lives. My lieutenant, for instance, is a man of wonderful courage and enterprise and the master is a man of excellent disposition, remarkable for his gentleness and the mildness of his discipline. My voyage is only delayed now because we are waiting for the weather to improve. The winter has been dreadfully severe but the spring promises well. Continue to write to me at every opportunity because your letters may arrive when my spirits most need reviving.
    Your affectionate brother, Robert Walton.

To Mrs Saville, England
7th July 1788

I write a few lines in haste to say that I am well advanced on my voyage. My men are bold and, apparently, of firm purpose. The floating sheets of ice that continually pass us do not appear to dismay them at all. We have already reached a high latitude but it is summer and, although not

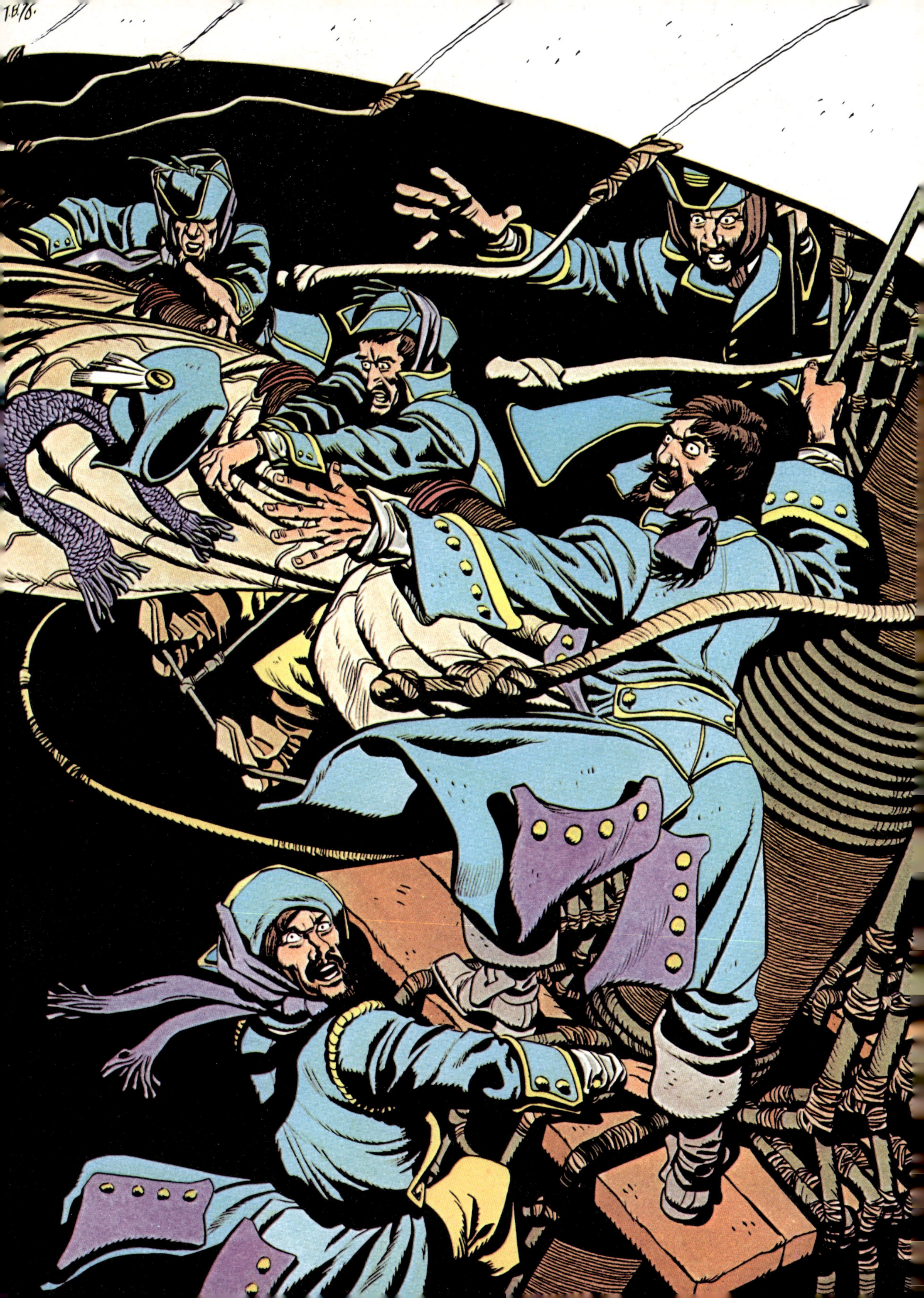
T.B/78.

so warm as in England, the southern gales bring a degree of renovating warmth which I had not expected. No untoward incidents have befallen us so far; one or two stiff gales and a leak in the hull are accidents to which experienced navigators attach little importance. I shall be well content if nothing worse happens during our voyage. Adieu, my dear Margaret. Be assured that, for my own sake as well as yours, I will not take unnecessary risks.
    Your affectionate brother, Robert Walton.

To Mrs Saville, England
5th August 1788

    Such a strange incident has occurred that I feel I must record it, even though it is probable that you will see me before this letter reaches you. Last Monday we were nearly surrounded by ice and very thick fog, and we lay to, hoping for a change in the weather. About two o'clock the mist cleared and we saw vast, irregular plains of ice stretching in every direction. Suddenly, a strange sight attracted our attention. We saw a low carriage, fixed on a sledge and drawn by dogs, pass by about half a mile north of the ship. Sitting in the sledge was a being which had the shape of a man but seemed to be of gigantic stature. We watched his progress through our telescopes until he was lost among the inequalities of the ice.

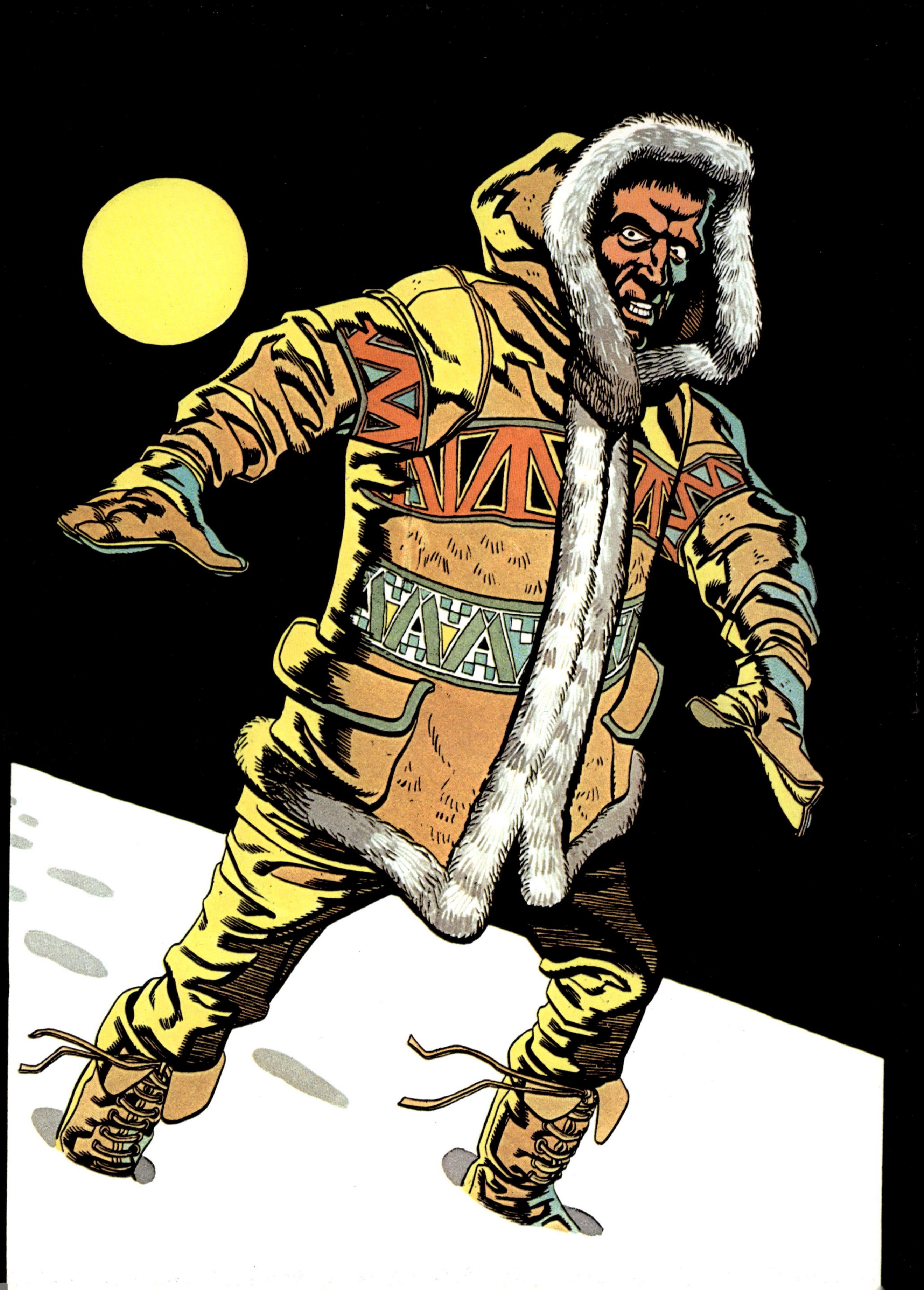

This occurrence excited our curiosity; we had thought that we were hundreds of miles from any land but it seemed that we were not. Two hours later the ice began to break up and the ship was free before nightfall. We decided, however, not to sail until the morning. When I went on deck the following day I found all the sailors on one side of the vessel, apparently talking to someone in the sea. A sledge, similar to the one which we had seen before, had drifted towards us during the night on a large fragment of ice. Only one of the dogs remained alive and there was a man in the sledge whom the sailors were persuading to come aboard. On seeing me, the stranger addressed me in English, although with a foreign accent.

'Before I come on board your vessel,' he said, 'will you have the kindness to inform me where you are going?'

I replied that we were on a voyage of discovery towards the North Pole. This appeared to satisfy him and he consented to come aboard. His limbs were nearly frozen and his body dreadfully emaciated by fatigue and suffering. We wrapped him in blankets and placed him near the galley stove. Slowly, he recovered and took a little soup, which restored him wonderfully.

After two days I removed him to a cabin and attended to him as much as my duties would permit. His eyes usually have an expression of wildness, even madness, about them but there are moments, after receiving some kindness, when his whole countenance lights up with unequalled benevolence and sweetness. I did my best to keep the men away from him so that he would not be tormented by their questions, for his state of mind and body dictate complete rest. Once, however, the lieutenant asked why he had come so far upon the ice in such a strange vehicle.

'To seek one who fled from me.'

'And did the man who you pursued travel in the same fashion?'

'Yes.'

'Then I think we have seen him, because the day before we picked you up, we saw some dogs drawing a sledge with a man in it.'

This aroused the stranger's interest, and he asked many questions about the route which the daemon, as he called him, had taken. A new spirit animated his decaying frame

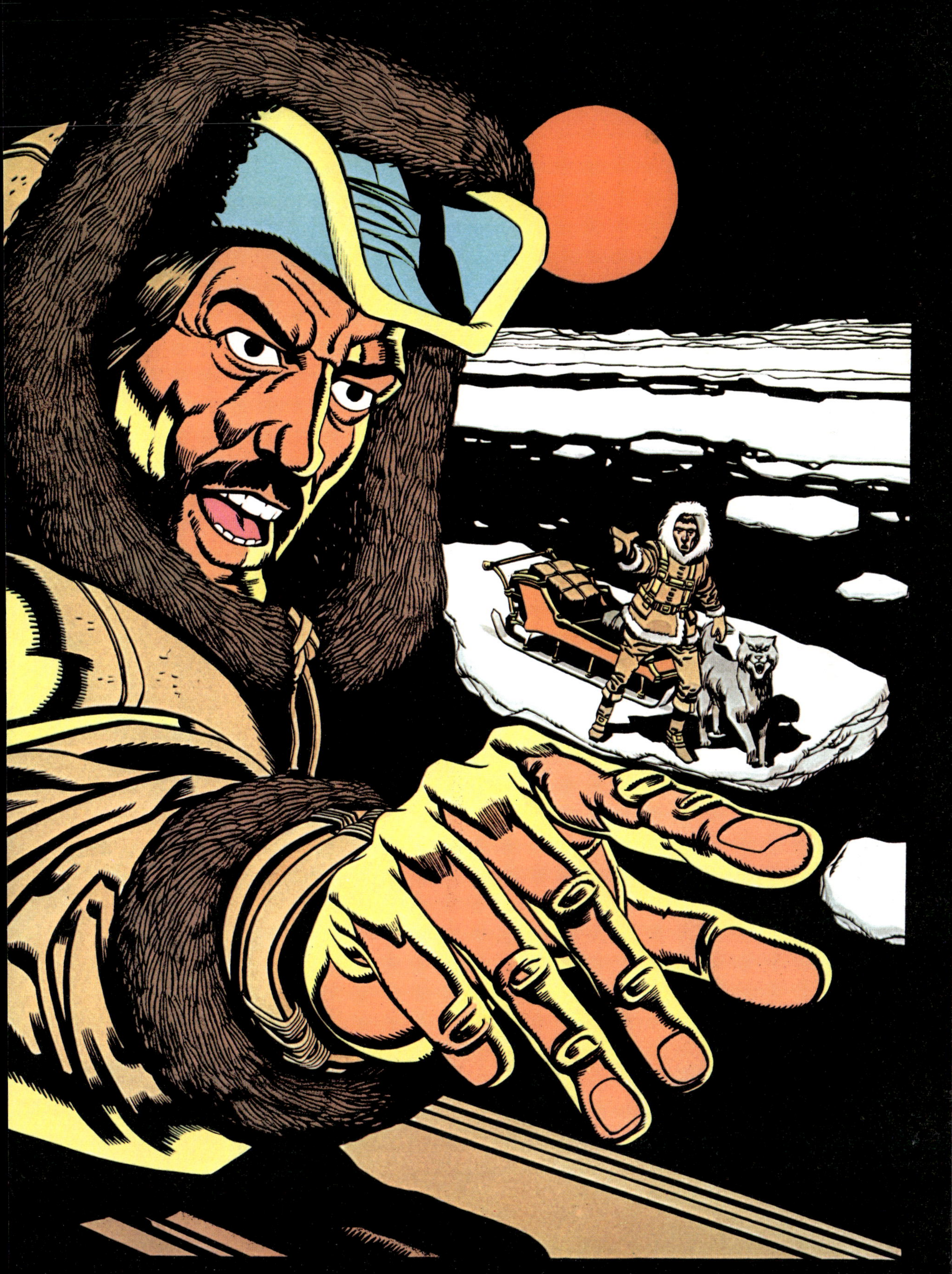

and he wanted to go on deck to watch for the sledge. I persuaded him to remain in the cabin, promising that someone would tell him if the sledge was sighted.

I said in one of my letters, my dear Margaret, that I should find no friend on the wide ocean and yet I have found a man who, before his spirit had been broken by misery, I should have been happy to have had as a close friend. I shall continue my account concerning him when I have fresh incidents to record.

Your affectionate brother, Robert Walton.

To Mrs Saville, England
13th August 1788

My affection for the stranger increases every day. He excites both my admiration and my pity; it grieves me to see such a noble creature destroyed by grief and yet he is gentle and wise, speaking with unparalleled eloquence. He has discussed my expedition with interest and I told him that I would gladly sacrifice my fortune, my life, my every hope to further my enterprise. At this, a dark gloom spread over his face; he placed his hands before his eyes and I saw tears trickling between his fingers. At length, he spoke:

'Unhappy man! Do you share my madness? Have you drunk also of the intoxicating draught? Let me reveal my tale and you will dash the cup from your lips!'

Later, when his emotional outburst had declined, I told him about my early years and my desire to find a friend with whom I would be in complete accord.

'I once had a friend,' he said, 'the most noble of human creatures and I am entitled, therefore, to judge as regards friendship. You have hope and the world before you, with no cause for despair. But I—I have lost everything and cannot begin life anew. You may easily perceive, Captain Walton, that I have suffered great misfortunes. I had decided at one time that the memory of these evils should die with me but I have changed my mind. You seek knowledge and wisdom as I once did and I hope that the gratification of your wishes may not be a serpent to sting you, as mine has been. You may draw a moral from my tale, that may direct you if you succeed or console you in case of failure.

Your affectionate brother, Robert Walton.

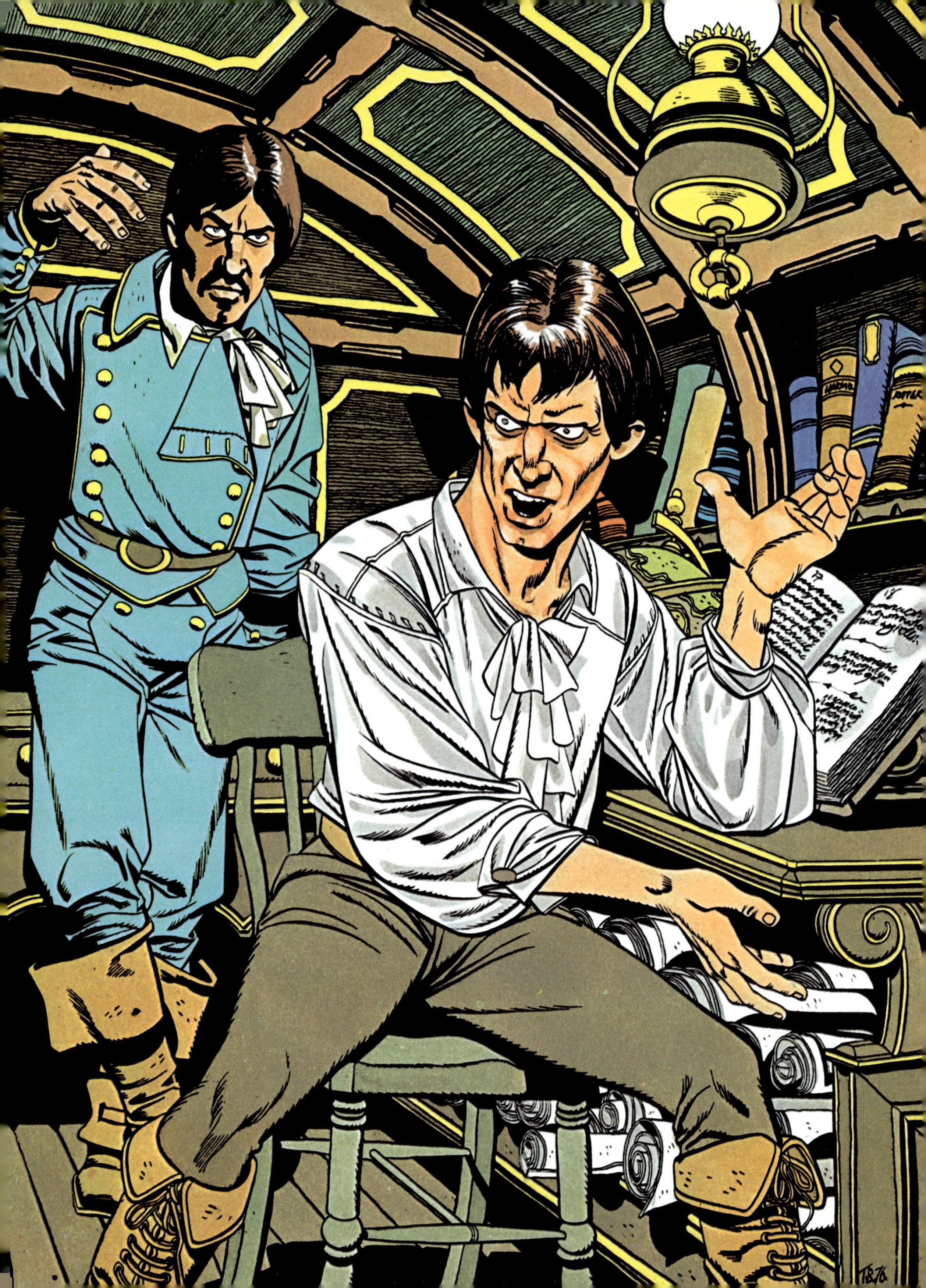

CHAPTER TWO

Victor Frankenstein's Story

I WAS born in Geneva; my father, Alphonse Frankenstein, was descended from a line of distinguished counsellors and magistrates. He himself had filled several public offices with distinction, being respected for his integrity and devotion to duty. A variety of circumstances conspired to prevent his marrying early and it was not until later in life that he became a husband and father. He married the daughter of a friend who died after he had fallen upon hard times; her name was Caroline Beaufort. There was a considerable difference between the ages of my parents but this seemed to bring them closer together in devoted affection.

When I was about five years old we were holidaying in Italy and spent a week on the shores of Lake Como and their benevolent disposition often made them visit the poor people of the district. One day they visited the house of a peasant couple who had, in addition to four children of their own, a young girl living with their family. She was thin and fair, her hair was the brightest gold, her brow was clear, her blue eyes cloudless and the moulding of her face so expressive of sensibility and sweetness that she seemed to have an almost celestial quality. She was the orphaned daughter of a Milanese aristocrat and my mother, with my father's permission, prevailed upon her guardians to yield their charge to her; they agreed as they saw that this would provide a greater opportunity for the girl. And so it was that Elizabeth Lavenza came into my parents' house, the beautiful and adored companion of all my occupations and pleasures.

On the birth of a second son, Ernest, my parents gave up the wandering life they had enjoyed since their marriage and settled again in Switzerland. We owned a house in Geneva and a country cottage at Belrive, on the shore of Lake Geneva. It was at Belrive that we spent most of our time and it was then that I met my greatest friend, Henry Clerval, the son of a merchant. He was a boy of singular talent who loved enterprise, hardship and even danger.

No-one could have passed a happier childhood than us: we felt that our parents were not tyrants but the agents and creators of the many delights which we enjoyed. Although my temper was sometimes violent and my passions vehement they were turned not towards childish pursuits but towards a desire to learn the secrets of heaven and earth, whether it was the outward substance of things or the inner spirit of nature and the mysterious soul of man.

When I was thirteen I first became acquainted with the works of Cornelius Agrippa, the cabbalist and occultist. My father advised me against reading them but I thought that he was not properly acquainted with their contents and ignored his advice. I continued to read avidly and acquired all Agrippa's writings as well as those of Paracelsus, the physician and alchemist, and Albertus Magnus, Aristotelian. I read and studied the wild fancies of these writers with delight, as I continued to penetrate the secrets of nature. Under the guidance of my new preceptors I entered with great diligence into the search for the philosopher's stone and the elixir of life.

When I was about fifteen years old we were staying at Belrive soon after the birth of my second brother, William. One night we witnessed a most violent and terrible thunderstorm which advanced from behind the mountains of Jura. The thunder burst at once with frightful loudness from various quarters of the heavens. As I stood at the door I beheld a sudden stream of fire issue from an old and beautiful oak which stood about twenty yards from our house. As soon as the dazzling light vanished, I saw that the oak had disappeared leaving only a blasted stump. When we inspected it more closely the next morning we found that it was not splintered by the shock but entirely reduced to thin ribbons of wood.

At the time of this occurrence, a man who had delved deeply into natural philosophy was staying with us and he explained a theory which he had formed on the subject of electricity and galvanism. I was familiar with the more obvious laws of electricity but what he said was both new and astonishing to me. All that he said threw Cornelius Agrippa and the other lords of my imagination into the shade. I lost the inclination to pursue my former studies and turned instead to mathematics. It was as if my guardian angel was trying to divert me from my earlier work and avert the storm that was hanging over me. But it was ineffectual since the immutable laws of Destiny had already decreed my utter and terrible destruction.

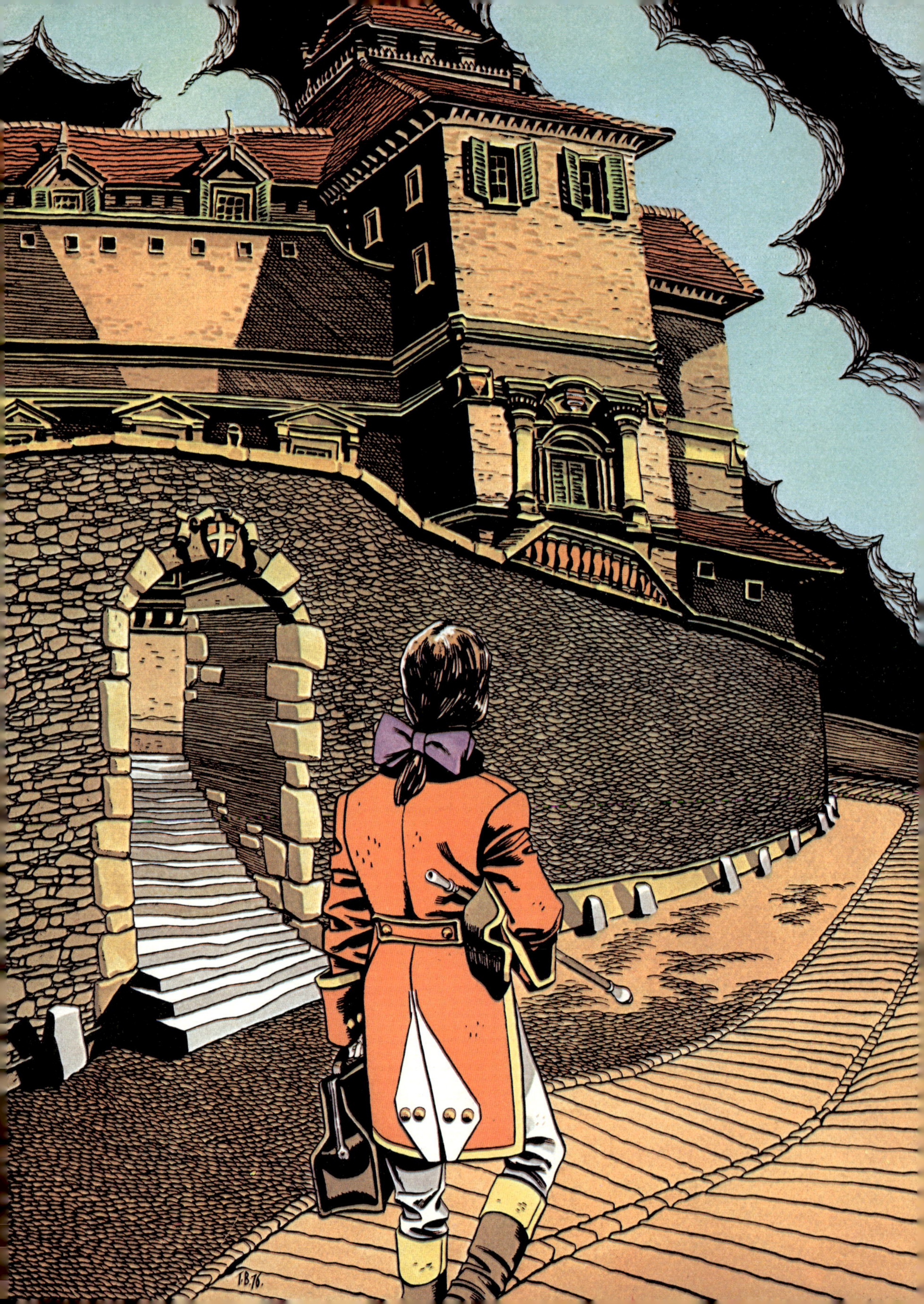

When I reached the age of seventeen, my parents decided that I should go to the University of Ingolstadt in Upper Bavaria. But before I departed, the first misfortune of my life occurred: an omen, as it were, of my future misery. Elizabeth had contracted scarlet fever and my mother insisted on caring for her, although we begged her to refrain. After three days she sickened herself and it was obvious that she would not survive the fever. On her death-bed she joined the hands of Elizabeth and myself together.

'My children,' she said, 'my firmest hopes of future happiness were placed on the prospect of your union. This expectation will now be the consolation of your father. Elizabeth, my love, you must take my place with the younger children. I regret that I am taken from you and, happy and beloved as I have been, it is hard to leave you all. But these are not thoughts befitting me; I will endeavour to resign myself cheerfully to death, and will indulge a hope of meeting you in another world.'

She died calmly and her countenance expressed affection even in death. It is so long before the mind can persuade itself that she whom we saw every day and whose very existence appeared part of our own, can have departed for ever. The brightness of a beloved eye had been extinguished and the sound of a familiar voice had been hushed for ever. My mother was dead but we still had to continue our lives, fortunate that our father still remained with us.

The day of my departure for Ingolstadt at length arrived and Henry Clerval spent the last evening with us. He had tried to persuade his father to permit him to accompany me but in vain. His father was a narrow-minded trader who saw only idleness and ruin in his son's aspirations. When I came down next morning to begin my journey, they were all there—my father to bless me, Clerval to press my hand once more, my Elizabeth to renew her entreaties that I would write often.

The journey to Ingolstadt was long and fatiguing and the high, white steeple of the town was a welcoming sight. I alighted from the chaise which had carried me from Geneva and was conducted to my apartment. It was situated on the dingy top floor of a building in the oldest part of the city, perched above a cliff which overlooked the dark waters of the Danube.

The following morning I delivered my letters of introduction and paid visits to some of the principal professors. Chance led me first to Mr Krempe, a professor of natural philosophy. He was an uncouth man but deeply imbued with the secrets of his science. He was astonished to learn that I had been studying Albertus Magnus and Paracelsus.

'Every instant that you have wasted reading those books is utterly and entirely lost. You have burdened your memory with exploded systems and useless names. My dear sir, you must begin your studies entirely anew.'

He gave me a list of several books dealing with natural philosophy which he said I should buy and informed me when his lectures would begin. He also mentioned the name of Mr Waldman, who would lecture upon chemistry. I spent the next two or three days becoming acquainted with the town and then decided to attend one of Mr Waldman's lectures. I was most favourably impressed by his bearing and his benevolent aspect, a contrast to the repulsive countenance of the squat Mr Krempe. I shall never forget his concluding remarks, a panegyric upon modern chemistry.

I did not close my eyes that night as my mind was in a state of turmoil. Eventually, near dawn, sleep came and when I awoke, yesterday's thoughts seemed like a dream. I paid Mr Waldman a visit and told him about my studies, asking him to advise me as to which books I ought to procure.

'I am happy,' said Mr Waldman, 'to have gained a disciple. If your wish is to become a man of science, and not merely a petty experimentalist, I should advise you to apply yourself to every branch of natural philosophy, including mathematics.'

He then took me into his laboratory and explained the uses of his various machines. He told me what I ought to obtain and promised that I would be able to use his equipment when I had advanced far enough so that I would not damage the mechanisms.

From that day natural philosophy, and particularly chemistry, became almost my sole occupation. I read

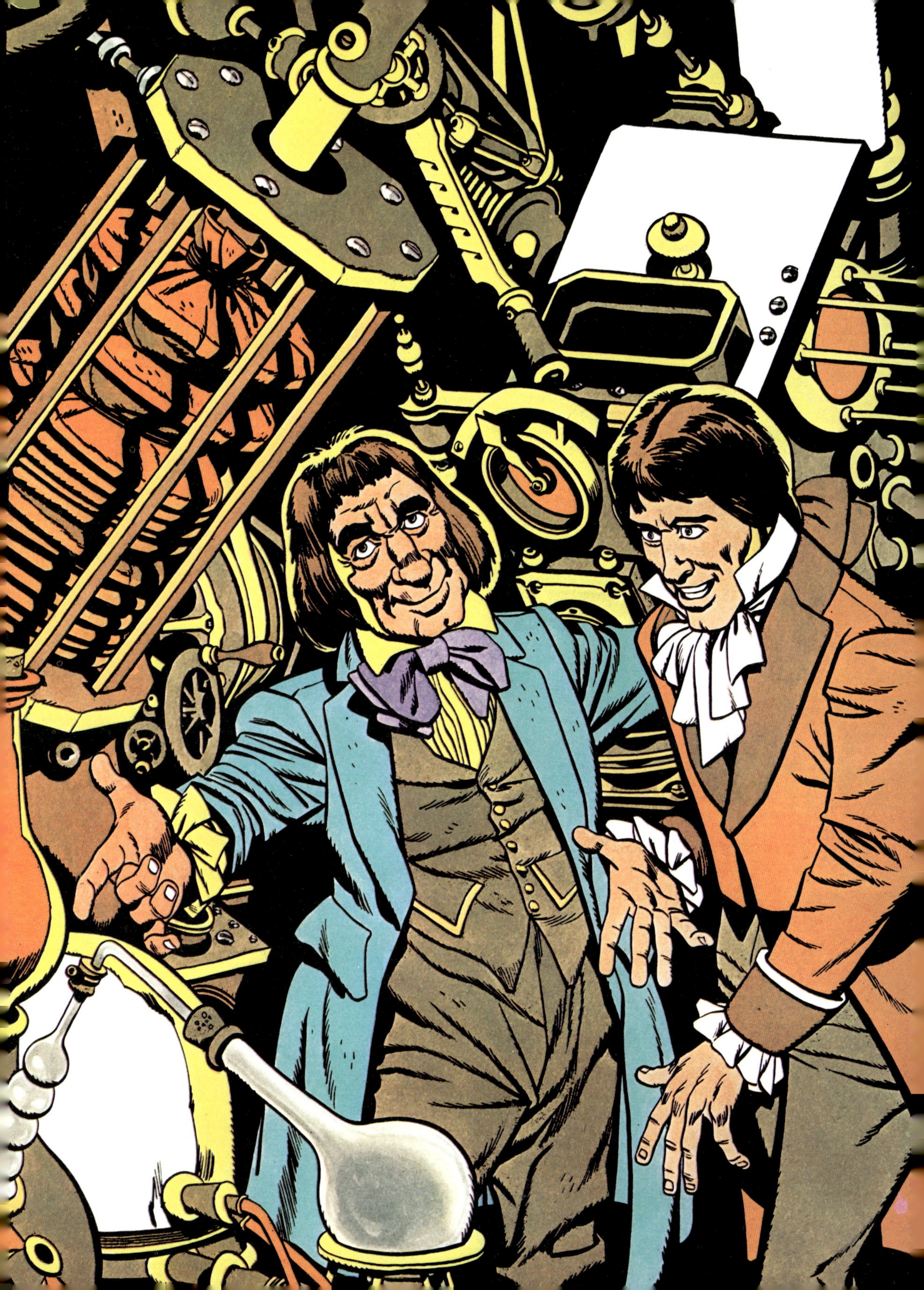

with ardour books written by modern researchers and attended lectures, cultivating the acquaintance of the University's men of science. I found even in Mr Krempe a great deal of sound sense and information, and in Mr Waldman I found a true friend. His gentleness was never tinged with dogmatism and his instructions were given with an air of frankness and good nature that banished every idea of pedantry. As I applied myself so closely to my studies, it may be understood that my progress was very rapid. My ardour and proficiency astonished not only the students but also my masters. Two years passed in this manner, during which I did not visit my father in Geneva but was engaged in the pursuit of some discoveries which I hoped to make.

At the end of the two years I thought of returning home but something happened which protracted my stay. One of the phenomena which had attracted my attention was the structure of the human frame and from whence the principle of life proceeded. Accordingly, I applied myself to physiology and became acquainted with the science of anatomy because, to examine the causes of life, we must first investigate death. I resolved to observe the natural decay and corruption of the human body and spent many days and nights in vaults and charnel-houses. I saw how the fine form of man was degraded and wasted, how the worm inherited the wonders of the eye and brain. I examined and analysed all the causes of the change from life to death and death to life, until from the midst of this darkness a sudden light broke in upon me—a light so brilliant and wondrous, yet so simple, that I became dizzy with the immensity of its implications. After days and nights of incredible labour and fatigue, I succeeded in discovering the cause of generation and life; more than that, I became capable of bestowing animation upon lifeless matter.

The astonishment which I experienced on first making this discovery soon gave way to delight and rapture. What had been the study and desire of the wisest men since the creation of the world was now within my grasp, a most gratifying consummation of my toils. When I found so astounding a power placed within my hands, I hesitated for a long time concerning the manner in which I

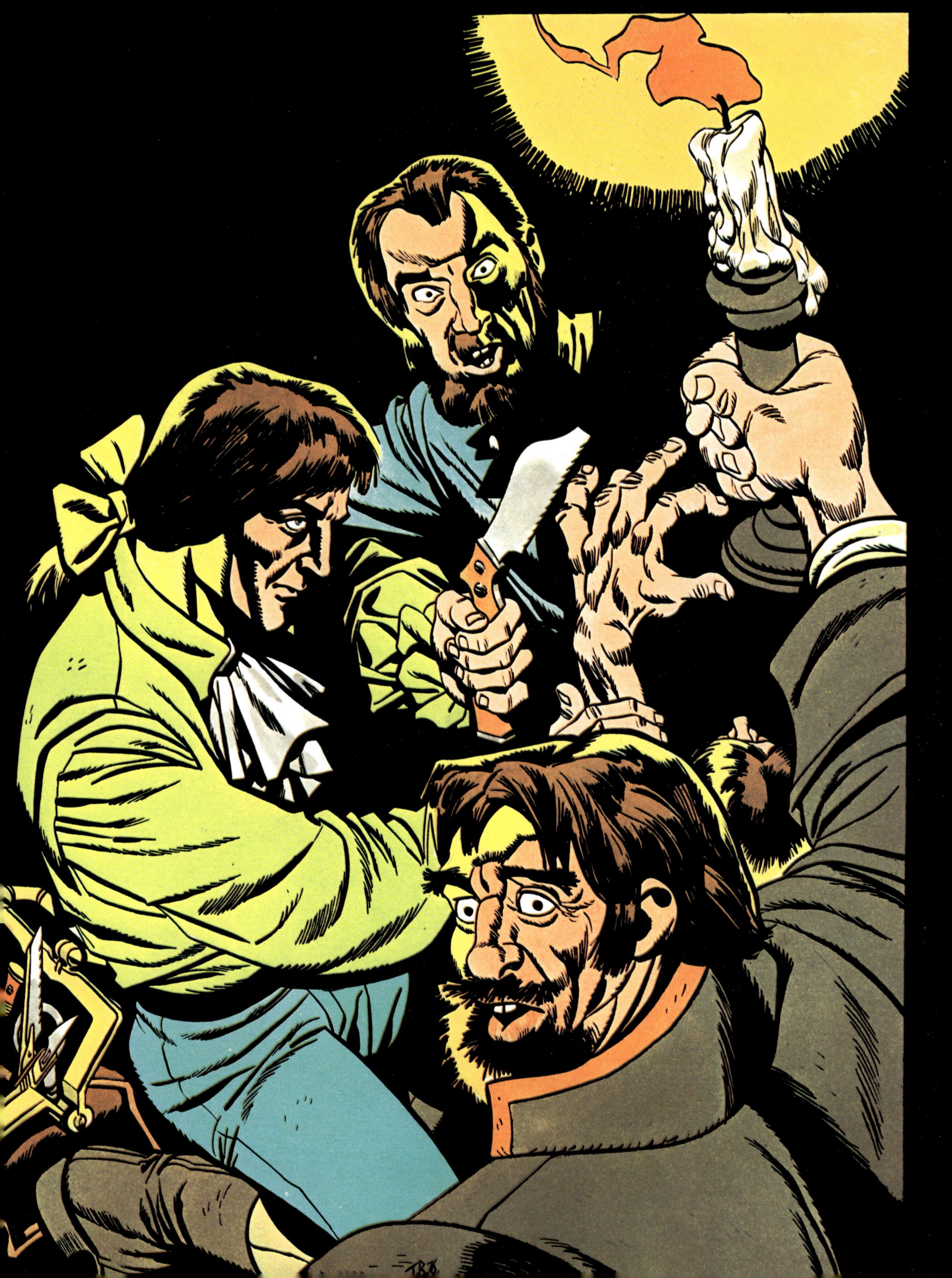

should employ it. Although I possessed the capacity of bestowing animation, to prepare a frame for the reception of it still remained a work of inconceivable difficulty. I wondered at first whether I should perhaps attempt the creation of an organism somewhat simpler than man but I was so exalted by my discovery as to cast aside all doubts of this kind and so I began the creation of a human being.

To ease my work, I decided to make the being of gigantic stature, about eight feet in height with matching proportions. I spent some months in collecting and arranging my materials, and then I began.

I pursued my undertaking with unremitting ardour, sustained by the thought that a new species would bless me as its creator and that I might, in time, renew life where death had apparently committed the body to corruption. Who, though, can conceive the horrors of my secret toil as I dabbled among the unhallowed dampness of the grave? I collected bones from charnel-houses and disturbed, with profane fingers, the tremendous secrets of the human frame. In a solitary chamber at the top of the building, I kept my workshop of filthy creation. The dissecting room and the slaughter-house furnished many of my materials and, although I often turned with loathing from my occupation, I was urged on by an increasing eagerness.

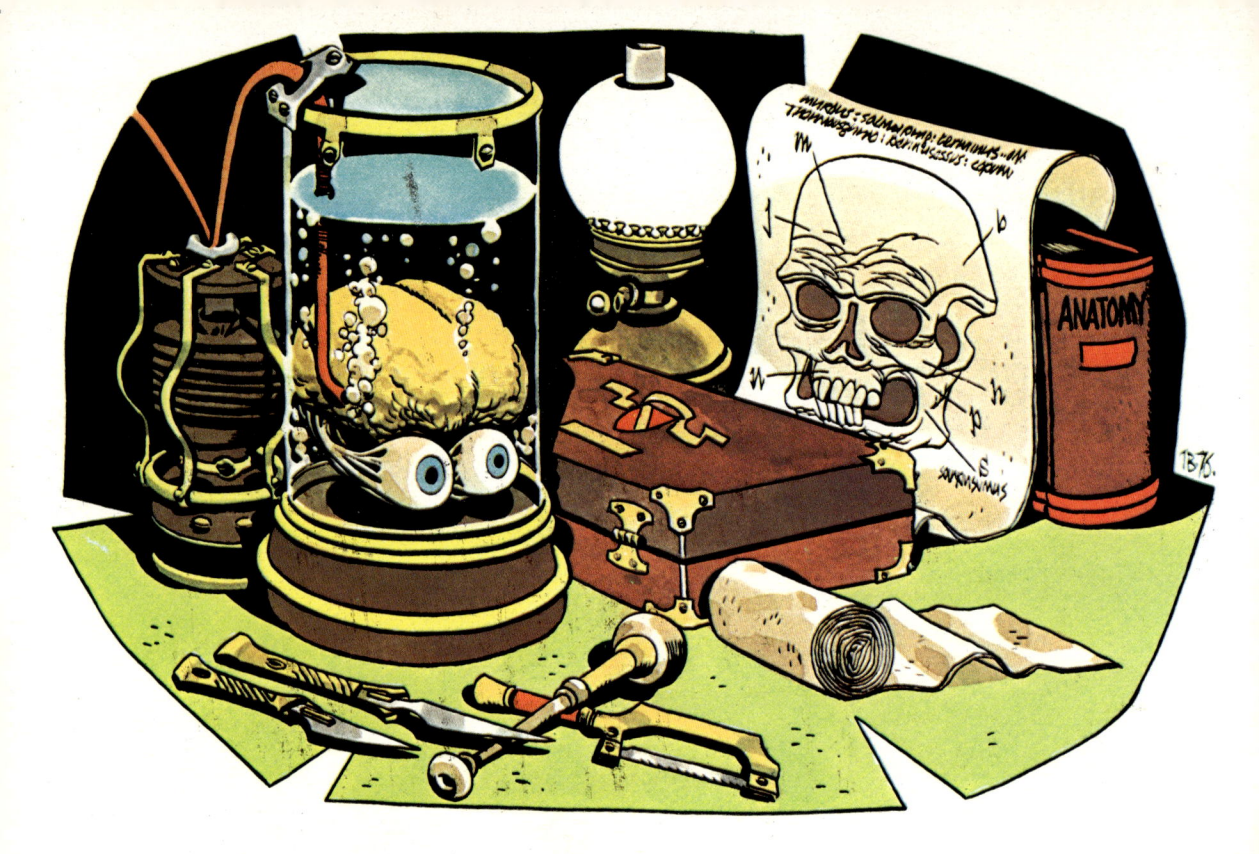

Winter, spring and summer passed away during my labours but I did not notice the changing seasons, so deeply was I engrossed in my task. The leaves of that year had withered before my work drew towards its close and every day showed me more plainly how well I had succeeded. Sometimes I grew alarmed at the wreck I had become but I promised myself both exercise and amusement when my labours were at an end.

❋ ❋ ❋ ❋

It was on a dreary November night that I beheld the fulfilment of my toils. At one in the morning I collected the instruments of life around me, to infuse the vital spark of being into the thing that lay at my feet. A cold wind blew down the Danube valley, heavy rain lashing

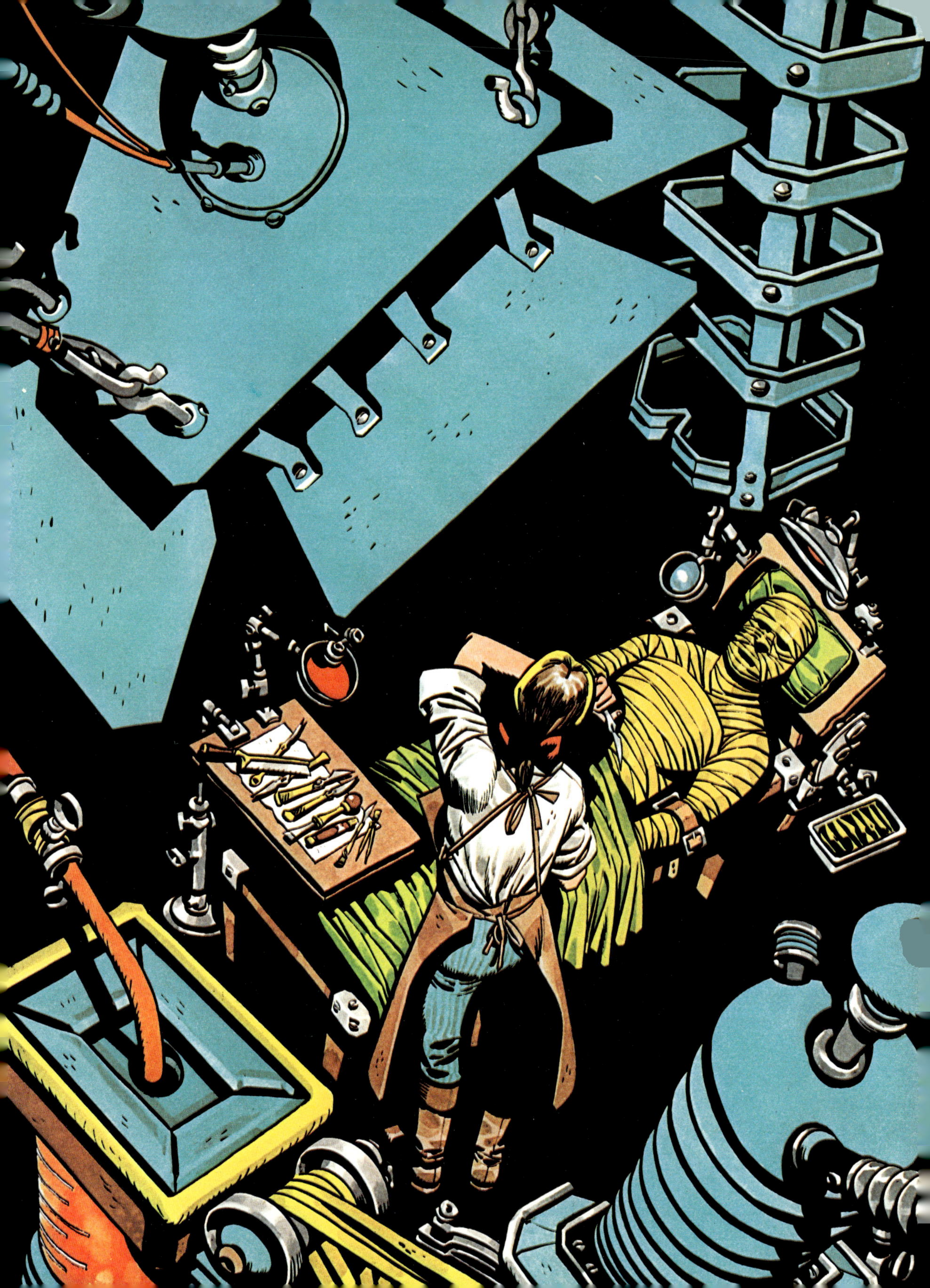

the window of my dark, cramped laboratory. As I made my final preparations, a great thunderstorm broke and tremendous flashes of lightning illuminated the creature who was soon to become a living being. I recalled the thunderstorm I had once watched in Geneva and how I had wondered at the power which the clouds contained. The teaching I had received concerning the theories of galvanism were now bearing fruit and, as my candle flickered dimly, I saw the dull yellow eye of the creature open; it breathed hard and a convulsive motion agitated its limbs.

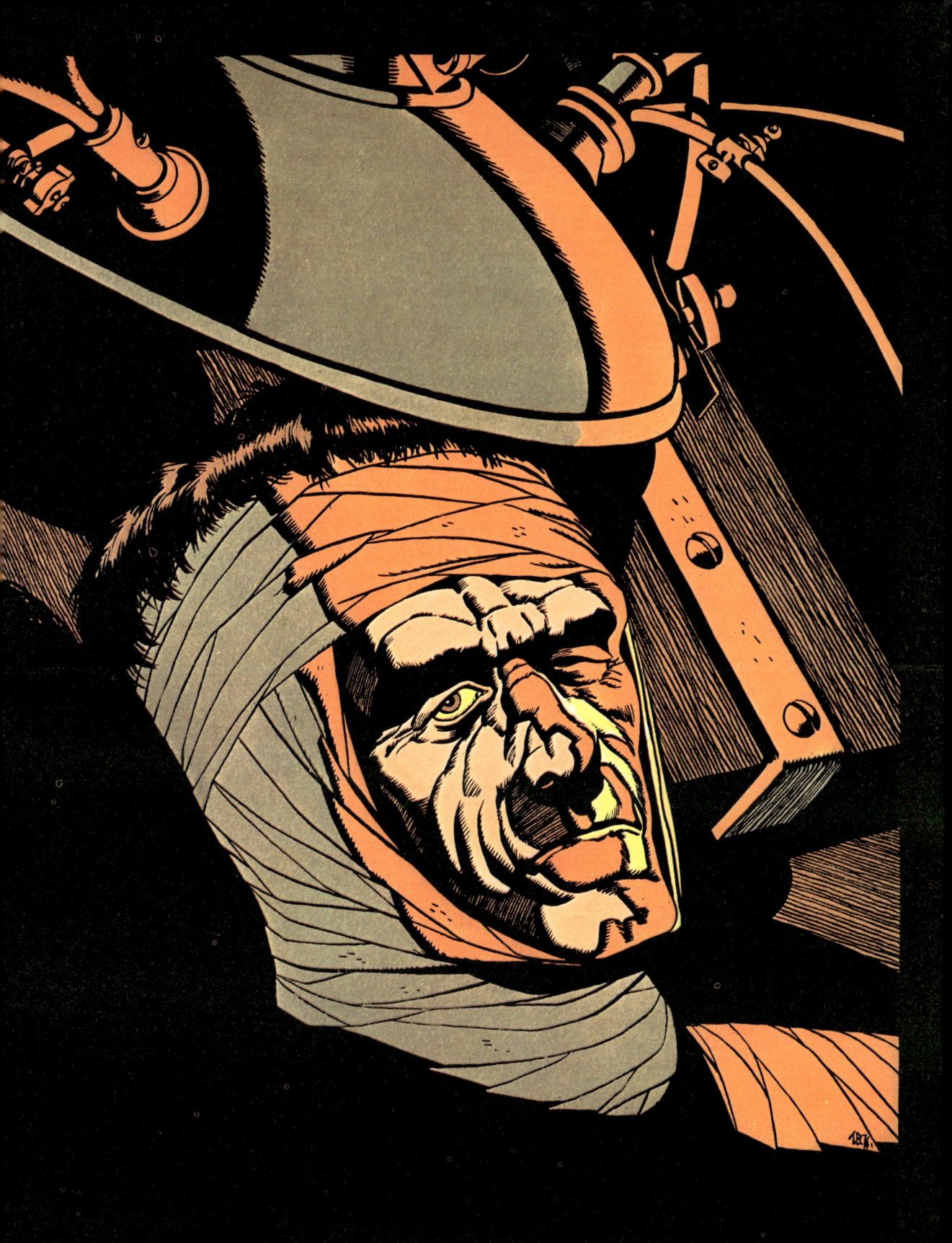

How can I describe my emotions at this catastrophe or describe the wretch whom, with such infinite pains and care, I had endeavoured to form? His limbs were in proportion and I had selected his features as beautiful. Beautiful! Great God! His yellow skin barely covered the work of the muscles and arteries beneath. His hair was of a lustrous black and his teeth were pearly white. But these luxuriances made a horrid contrast with his watery eyes, his shrivelled complexion and straight black lips.

I had worked hard for nearly two years with the sole purpose of infusing life into an inanimate body. But now that I had finished, the beauty of my dream had vanished and horror and disgust filled my heart. Unable to endure the sight of the being I had created, I rushed out of the room. For a long time I paced my bedroom, unable to sleep. I threw myself on the bed, still fully dressed, and slept only fitfully. I was disturbed by the wildest dreams: I thought I saw Elizabeth walking in the streets of Ingolstadt. Delighted, I embraced her but as we kissed, her features began to change and I thought that I held the corpse of my dead mother in my arms. I started from my sleep, my teeth chattering and every limb convulsed. By the light of the moon I beheld the wretch, the miserable monster whom I had created. He held up the curtain of the bed, his eyes fixed upon me. He muttered some inarticulate sounds while a grin wrinkled his cheek. One hand was held out, seemingly to detain me, but I escaped and took refuge in the courtyard below where I remained during the rest of the night.

At length, morning dawned, dismal and wet. At six o'clock the porter opened the gates of the courtyard and I walked the streets without any clear conception of where I was or what I was doing. I came at length to an inn where carriages usually stopped and saw a Swiss coach coming towards me. It stopped just by me and, as the door opened, I saw my friend Henry Clerval.

'My dear Frankenstein!' he exclaimed. 'How glad I am to see you! How lucky that you should be here at this moment.'

I felt suddenly, for the first time in many months, a calm and serene joy. I welcomed him in the most cordial manner and we walked towards my apartment.

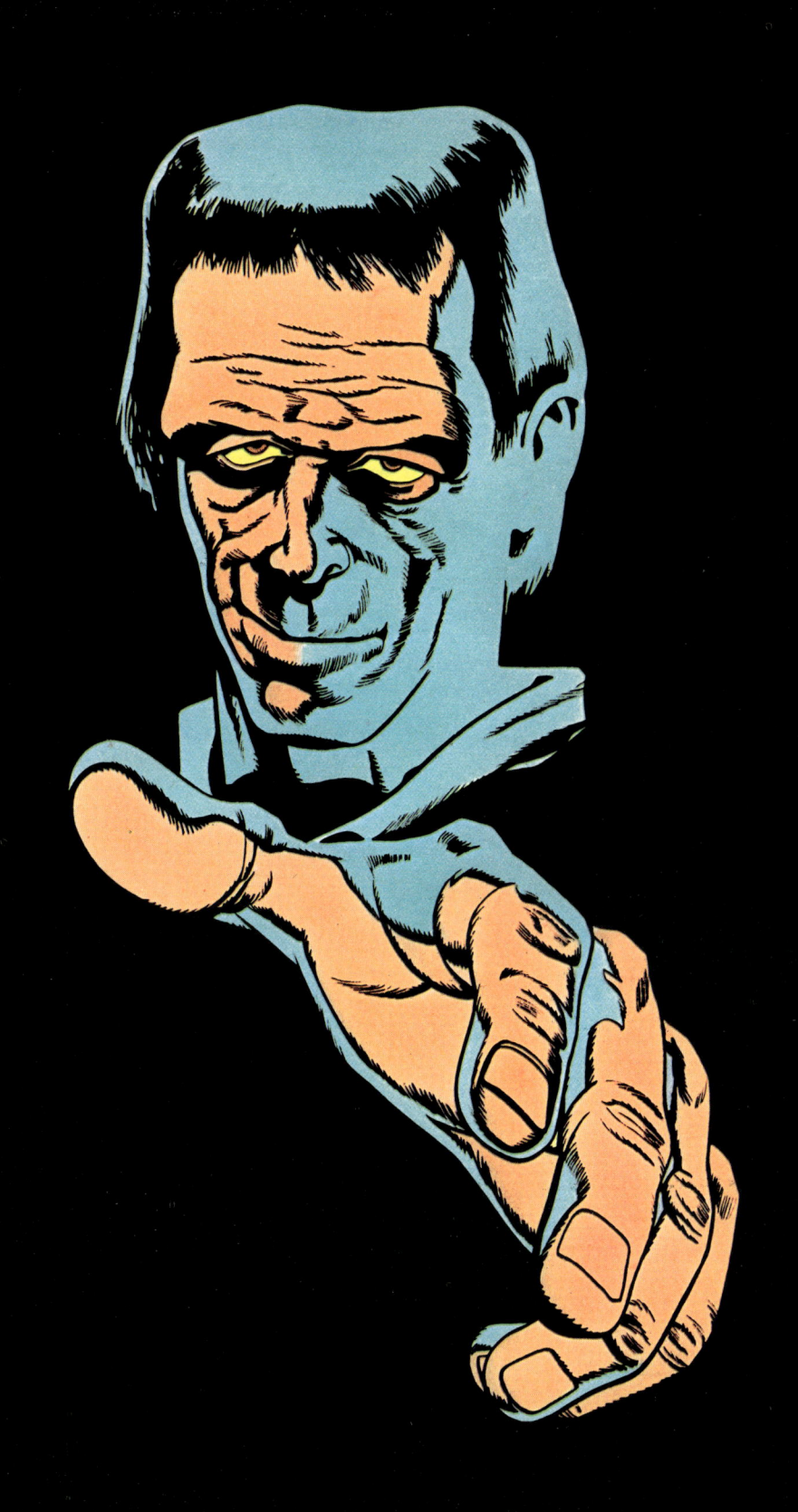

'You will realise,' he said, 'how difficult it was to persuade my father that not all knowledge was to be found in the noble art of book-keeping. But his affection for me overcame his prejudice and he has permitted me to undertake a voyage of discovery to the land of learning.'

He was able to tell me that my family were well but anxious to receive a letter from me. He remarked on my haggard appearance and I explained that I had been deeply engaged in one occupation and not allowed myself sufficient rest. When we arrived at my rooms I asked Henry to wait below and darted upstairs. I stepped fearfully in: the place was empty, my hideous guest had gone. I could hardly believe that such good fortune had befallen me and I ran down to fetch Clerval. I was unable to contain myself and jumped over the chairs, clapping my hands and laughing aloud. Clerval observed a wildness in my eyes for which he could not account.

'My dear Victor,' he cried, 'what for God's sake is the matter? Do not laugh in that manner. What is the cause of all this?'

'Do not ask me,' I cried, putting my hands before my eyes for I thought I saw the dreaded spectre enter the room. I imagined that the monster seized me and I fell upon the floor, struggling furiously. This was the commencement of a nervous fever which lasted for many months. During that time Henry was my only nurse and he kept from my family the extent of my illness. By the time I had recovered it was spring and Henry gave me a letter from Elizabeth which had arrived a few days earlier.

My Dearest Cousin,

You have been very ill and even the constant letters from dear, kind Henry are not sufficient to reassure me. My persuasions have restrained your father from undertaking the inconvenient and, perhaps, dangerous journey to Ingolstadt. Clerval writes that you are getting better and I eagerly hope that you will confirm this soon in your own handwriting. Get well—and return to us. How pleased you would be to see the progress that Ernest has made! He is now sixteen and wishes to enter into foreign service, like a true Swiss. I must also say a few words to you, my dear cousin, of darling little William. He is very tall for

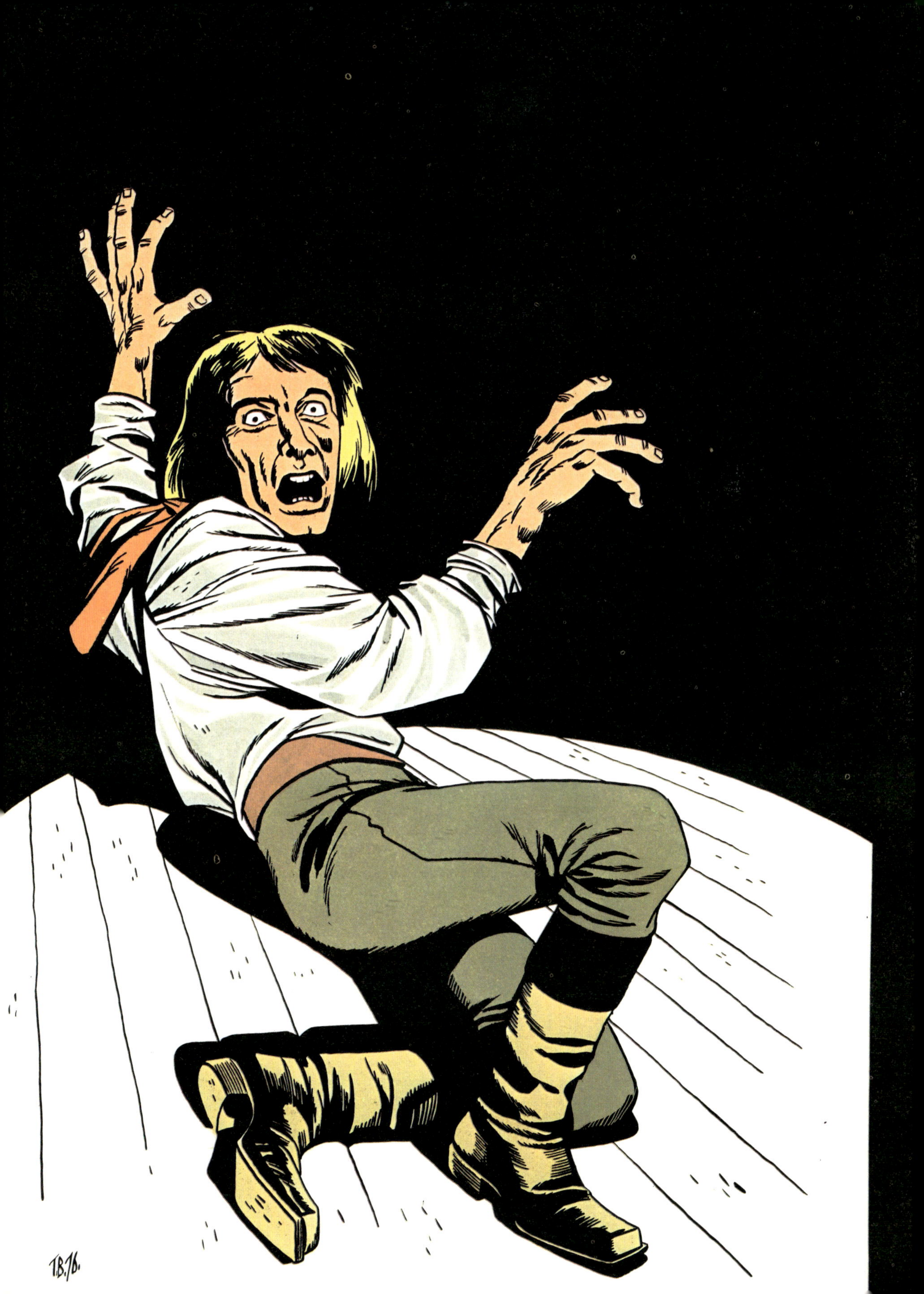
T.B.76.

his age, with sweet laughing blue eyes, dark eyelashes and curling hair. When he smiles, two little dimples appear on each rosy cheek.

Ten thousand thanks to Henry for his kindness and his letters. Adieu, my cousin. I entreat you, write!

Elizabeth Lavenza.

I wrote to Elizabeth immediately and, two weeks later when my strength had returned, I began introducing Clerval to several professors at the University. Clerval had never shared my taste for natural philosophy and had come to the University with the intention of studying oriental languages. Now that I wished to fly from my former studies, I decided to join him in his work. I did not, like him, attempt a critical knowledge of their dialects but read merely to understand their meaning for temporary amusement.

The summer passed pleasantly and I had intended to return to Geneva in the autumn but I procrastinated and the winter arrived, retarding my journey until the following spring. In May, Henry proposed a walking tour of the district before I went home and, accordingly, we spent two weeks exploring the surrounding countryside. We returned to the University on a Sunday afternoon and my spirits were high as I bounded along with feelings of unbridled joy and hilarity.

* * * *

On my return, I found the following letter from my father.

My dear Victor,

You have probably waited impatiently for a letter to fix the date of your return to us and I was tempted only to write a few lines, mentioning the day on which I would expect you. But it would be cruel to allow you to expect a happy welcome when you would find only tears.

William is dead! That sweet child, whose smiles delighted and warmed my heart. Victor, he is murdered!

Last Thursday, I went walking with Elizabeth and your two brothers. As it was pleasant weather, we prolonged our walk and Ernest and William had gone ahead. Presently, Ernest came back saying that William had playfully run away to hide and that he could not be found. We searched for him until night fell and then continued with torches. About five in the morning I discovered my lovely boy, stretched on the grass livid and motionless, the print of the murderer's finger on his neck.

Elizabeth was distraught because a miniature of your mother which she had let William wear was gone and she feared that it was this which tempted the perpetrator of this foul deed. Come home, dearest Victor, for you alone can console her.

Your affectionate and afflicted father,
Alphonse Frankenstein.

I threw the letter on the table, and covered my face with my hands.

'My dear Frankenstein,' exclaimed Henry. 'What has happened?'

I handed him the letter and tears sprang from his eyes too as he read my father's story.

'What do you intend to do?' he asked.

'Go instantly to Geneva. Come with me, Henry, to order the horses.'

My journey was very melancholy and I could hardly sustain the multitude of feelings that crowded into my mind. It was dark when I reached Geneva and the gates were already shut. I was forced to spend the night at Secheron, a village near the city. As I was unable to rest, I decided to visit the spot where poor William had been murdered. As I neared the place, large drops of rain began to fall and thunder crashed overhead. The rain became heavier but I walked on, watching the storm playing around the mountains that bordered Lake Geneva.

Then I saw a figure which stole from behind a clump of trees not far from me. I gazed intently, fixed to the spot. Its gigantic stature and deformity of aspect could not be mistaken: it was the wretch, the filthy daemon to whom I had given life. What was he doing there? Could he have murdered my brother? No sooner did the idea cross my mind than I became convinced that it was the truth. The figure passed me quickly and was lost in the gloom. I thought of following him but a flash of lightning showed him climbing the nearly perpendicular rocks of Mont Saleve. He soon reached the summit and disappeared.

No one can conceive the anguish which I suffered during the rest of the night, which I spent, cold and wet, in the open air. But the weather did not trouble me as my imagination was busy in scenes of evil and despair. At dawn, I walked towards the city and hastened to my father's house, waiting in the library until the family rose. I had considered, since I felt I knew the identity of the murderer, telling my father about the creature which I had made. But I reflected that if anyone else had told me such a tale, I should have thought them insane. And what would be the use of pursuit? Who could catch a creature capable of scaling the overhanging sides of Mont Saleve?

Ernest entered the room to welcome me.

'My dearest Victor,' he said, 'your presence will, I hope, revive our father who seems to be sinking beneath his misfortune.'

'And what of Elizabeth?' I asked.

'She requires consolation most of all,' he answered. 'Your influence will, I hope, induce her to stop her vain and tormenting self-accusations. The death of our brother

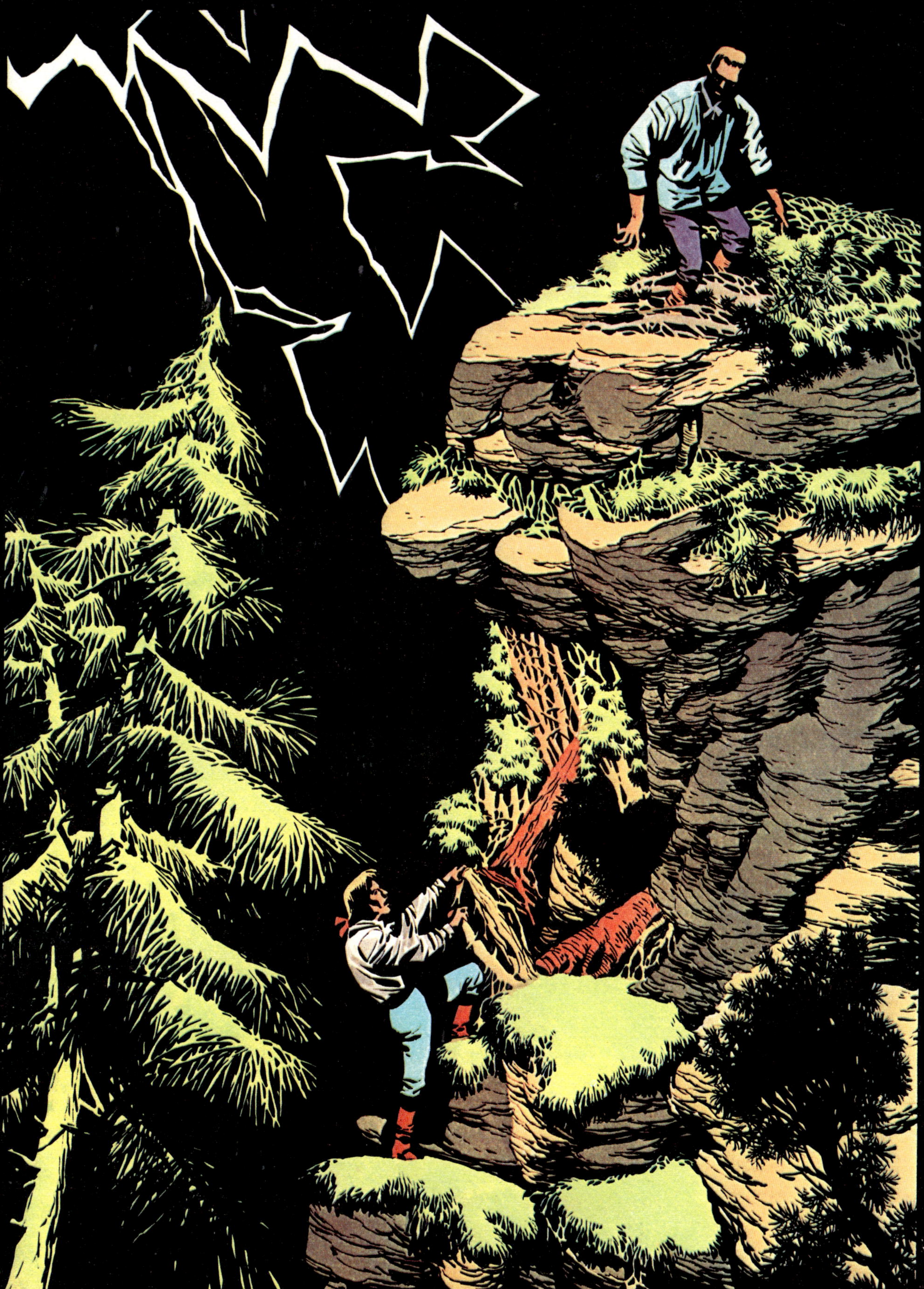

has made her very unhappy. But since the murderer has been discovered . . .'

'Discovered! Good God, how can that be? It is impossible; one might as well try to overtake the winds, or confine a mountain stream with a straw. I saw him: he was free last night.'

'I don't know what you mean,' said Ernest. 'No-one would believe at first that Justine Moritz, so amiable and fond of all the family, was capable of this frightful crime.'

I could scarcely comprehend his words. Justine Moritz, another orphan girl who my father had taken into our home and who was like a sister to us all? She could not have harmed darling William! Ernest explained that, on the day after William's murder, the miniature picture of my mother, which he had been wearing, was found in her pocket. The servant who discovered it went to a magistrate and Justine was arrested.

'You are all mistaken', I said. 'Poor, good Justine is innocent.'

At that moment, my father entered the room and, despite his sadness, tried to welcome me cheerfully. He told me that Justine was to be tried that day but I was so convinced that she was innocent that I was certain that not enough circumstantial evidence could be brought forward to convict her. At that instant, Elizabeth joined us.

'Your arrival, my dear cousin,' she said, 'fills me with hope. You, perhaps, will find some way to save Justine. If she is condemned, I shall never know joy again.'

'She is innocent, my Elizabeth,' I said, 'and that shall be proved.'

'How kind and generous you are!' she exclaimed. 'Every one else believes in her guilt and to see people so prejudiced makes me despair.'

The trial began at eleven o'clock, my father and the rest of the family being obliged to attend as witnesses. I accompanied them to the court and suffered living torture during this wretched mockery of justice. A thousand times I wished I had confessed myself to be guilty of the crime but I was absent when it was committed and such a declaration would have been considered to be little better than the ravings of a madman.

    Several witnesses were called by the prosecution and it was said that Justine had been out the whole of the night of the murder. When shown the body, she had fallen into violent hysterics and was kept in bed for several days. Although Justine had begun the trial in a composed state, as it progressed surprise, horror and misery were all strongly expressed on her face. She explained how she had visited an aunt during the day and had been shut out of the city at night, sleeping in a barn. She also said that, both in the morning and previous evening, she had been looking for William, whose disappearance she had heard of from a passer-by. A number of people were called to speak for her but they were afraid to come forward because of the nature of the crime she was said to have committed. Only Elizabeth was willing to speak and describe how good and kind Justine was.

My own agitation and anguish was extreme during the whole trial. I believed in her innocence and could not sustain the horror of my situation. Could the daemon who murdered my brother also have betrayed Justine? The next morning I went to the court, my lips and throat parched. I dared not ask the fatal question but I was known and the officer guessed the reason for my visit.

The ballots had been thrown and Justine was condemned. I was told that she had confessed to the crime and that she wished to see Elizabeth.

I accompanied Elizabeth to the prison and found Justine sitting on some straw, her hands manacled. She threw herself at Elizabeth's feet, weeping bitterly. My cousin wept also.

'I did confess,' cried Justine, 'but I confessed a lie. I confessed that I might obtain absolution but now that falsehood lies heavier on my heart than all my other sins. Dear William! I shall see you soon in Heaven, where we shall all be happy.'

Elizabeth, who was much distressed, proclaimed her intention to prove Justine's innocence, but Justine said that she did not fear death since God gave her courage to endure the worst. As we prepared to leave, she assumed an air of cheerfulness and embraced Elizabeth.

'Farewell, sweet lady,' she said. 'May Heaven, in its bounty, bless and preserve you. May this be the last misfortune that you will ever suffer. Live and be happy, and make others so.'

And on the morrow, Justine died.

✸ ✸ ✸ ✸

About this time we retired to our house at Belrive. Often, after the rest of the family had gone to bed, I took the boat out and passed many hours upon the water. I was often tempted to plunge into the silent lake so that the water might close over me and my troubles for ever. But I was restrained by the thought of Elizabeth, who I loved tenderly and whose existence was bound up in mine. And I was afraid that, if I left them, my family would be exposed to the malice of the fiend that I had let loose among them. My abhorrence of this fiend cannot be conceived: I ardently wished to extinguish that life which I had so thoughtlessly bestowed. I wished to see him again that I might avenge the deaths of William and Justine.

My father's health was deeply shaken by the horror of recent events and Elizabeth was sad and despondent, taking no delight in her ordinary occupations. She was no longer that happy creature who had talked with ecstasy of our future prospects.

'There is an expression of despair, dear Victor, in your countenance that makes me tremble,' she said. 'Banish those dark passions and remember the friends around you. Have we lost the power to make you happy?'

But the tenderness of friendship could not redeem my

soul from woe; the very accents of love were ineffectual. Sometimes the passions which overwhelmed me drove me to seek some relief from my intolerable sensations. It was during one of these tortured periods that I left my home for a while and journeyed to Chamounix in the French Alps. The valley of Chamounix is wonderful and sublime, bounded by snowy mountains with immense glaciers approaching the road. I heard the rumbling of an avalanche and saw the supreme magnificence of Mont Blanc which overlooked the valley.

   I spent the night at the village of Chamounix and the following day I went roaming through the valley. Although the rain was pouring in torrents and thick mists hid the summits of the mountains, I resolved to ascend to the top of Montanvert. The climb was precipitous, the path being intersected by ravines of snow, down which stones continually rolled. It was almost noon when I arrived at the top; for some time I sat upon a rock overlooking the sea of ice, winding among the mountains.

Presently, I descended to the glacier and spent the next two hours crossing its uneven surface, which was interspersed with deep crevasses. As I sheltered in a recess of the rock, gazing on this wonderful scene, I suddenly beheld the figure of a man coming towards me at superhuman speed. I could see that his stature seemed to exceed that of man: a mist came over my eyes and I felt a faintness seize me. I perceived as the shape came nearer that it was the wretch I had created. I trembled with rage, resolving to wait his approach and engage him in mortal combat. His countenance bespoke bitter anguish while its unearthly ugliness rendered it almost too horrible for human eyes.

'Devil!' I exclaimed. 'Do you dare approach me? Do you not fear the vengeance I may wreak on your miserable head? Oh, that I could, by extinguishing your existence,

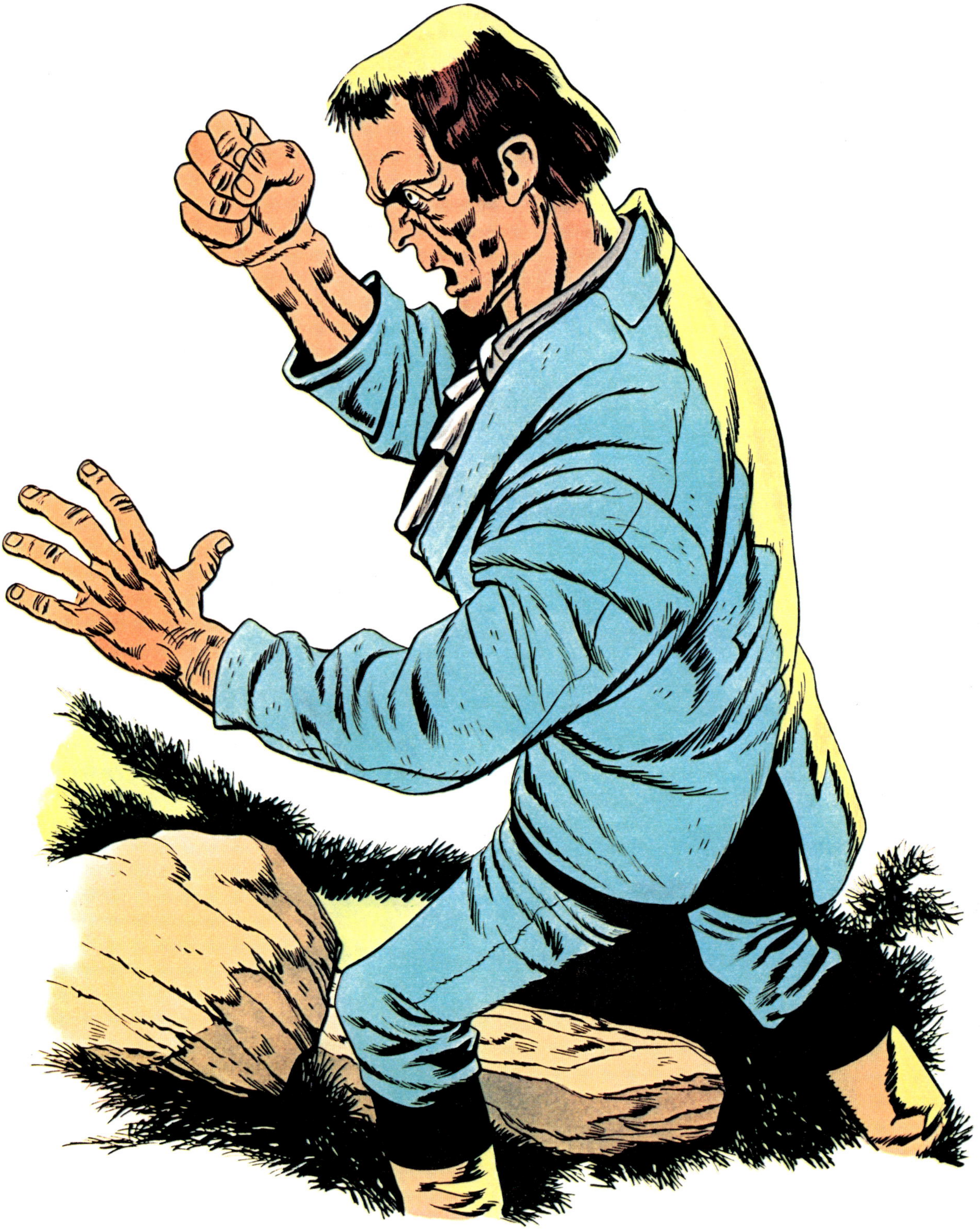

restore those victims whom you have so diabolically murdered!'

'I expected your anger,' said the daemon. 'All men hate the wretched and I am miserable beyond all living things. Even you, who created me, detest me. You are bound to me by ties which only the death of one of us will break. Do your duty towards me and I will do mine towards you and the rest of mankind. If you will agree to my conditions, I will leave them and you at peace. If you refuse I will swamp the jaws of death with the blood of your family and friends.'

My rage was without bounds and I sprang at him but he easily eluded me, saying:

'Be calm! I beg you to hear me. Have I not suffered enough without you wishing to increase my misery? Although life is nothing but anguish to me, I will defend it. Remember, I am your creature and although you have made me more powerful than yourself I will be docile if you will make me happy.'

'Begone! I will not listen,' I said. 'There can be no communication between us for we are enemies.'

'Will nothing I say cause you to look favourably upon me? Believe me, Frankenstein, I was benevolent: my soul glowed with love and humanity and yet you, and your fellow creatures, abhor me. The deserted mountains and dreary glaciers are my refuge. Listen to my tale and when you have heard it either abandon or help me, as you judge that I deserve.'

'Why do you remind me,' I rejoined, 'of those awful circumstances, that dreadful day in which you first saw light? Cursed be the hands that formed you! You have left me no power to consider whether I am just to you or not.'

'Hear my story: it is long and strange. The sun is high in the heavens, but before it sets you will have heard my tale and can decide. The temperature of this place is not right for you: come to the hut upon the mountain.'

He led the way across the ice and I followed. We climbed the opposite rock and entered the rough hut in which he lived. My heart was heavy but I agreed to hear him out and seated myself by the fire which my odious companion had lit.

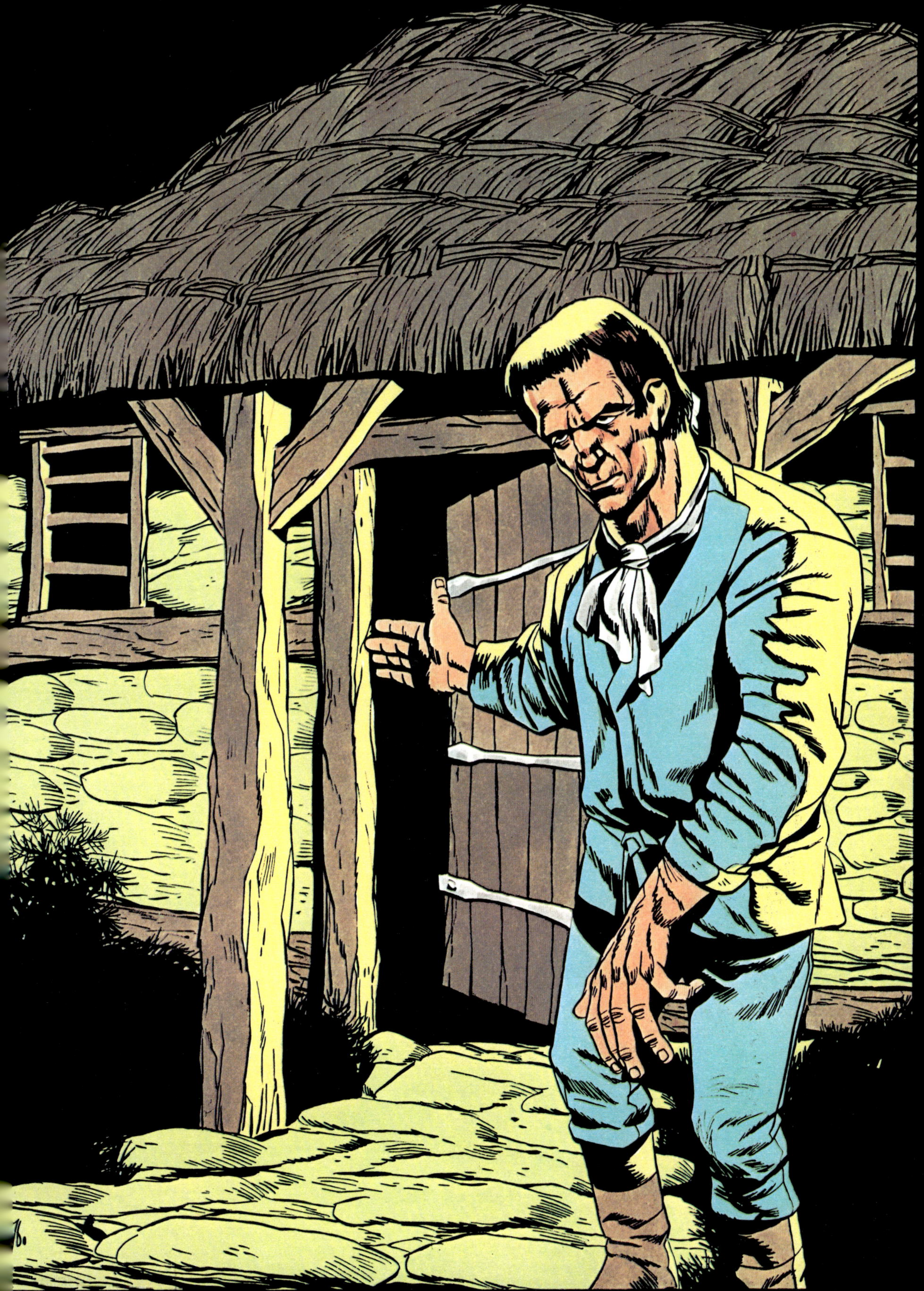

CHAPTER THREE

The Creature's Story

I CANNOT recall the earliest moments of my being as the events of that period are confused and indistinct. I walked and, I believe, I descended. The light became more and more oppressive and the heat wearied me as I walked. I found a shady place in the forest near Ingolstadt and rested by the side of a brook. I was hungry and thirsty, so I ate berries which I found hanging on trees and drank from the brook.

I slept for a while and awoke feeling cold. Although I had taken some clothes before leaving your rooms, they did not keep me warm at night. I was a poor, helpless, miserable wretch able only to feel pain invading me on all sides. I sat down and wept. Several days and nights passed and I began to learn more of my surroundings, finding pleasure in the songs of the birds and the green leaves of the trees. My eyes became accustomed to the light and I began to see forms properly, being able to tell the difference between insects and plants.

One day, when suffering from the cold, I found a fire left by some wandering beggars and was delighted at the warmth which came from it. I was able to put more wood on the fire and learnt to keep it burning. But food was scarce and I decided to move on and find a place where my wants could be more easily satisfied. After three days I reached open country which was covered in snow. My feet were chilled by it and I longed for food and shelter. I saw a small hut and, finding the door open, I went in. An old man sat near the fire, preparing his breakfast. He heard me enter, turned, shrieked loudly and fled. His flight surprised me but I liked the hut and decided to stay there for a while. I ate the food which he had left and fell asleep on some straw.

Later, I left the hut and walked across fields for several hours until I came to a village. It seemed quite wonderful to me with the neat cottages, an inn and stately houses. There were vegetables in the gardens, milk and cheese at some of the windows. My appetite was roused by the sight of all this food and I stepped into one of the cottages.

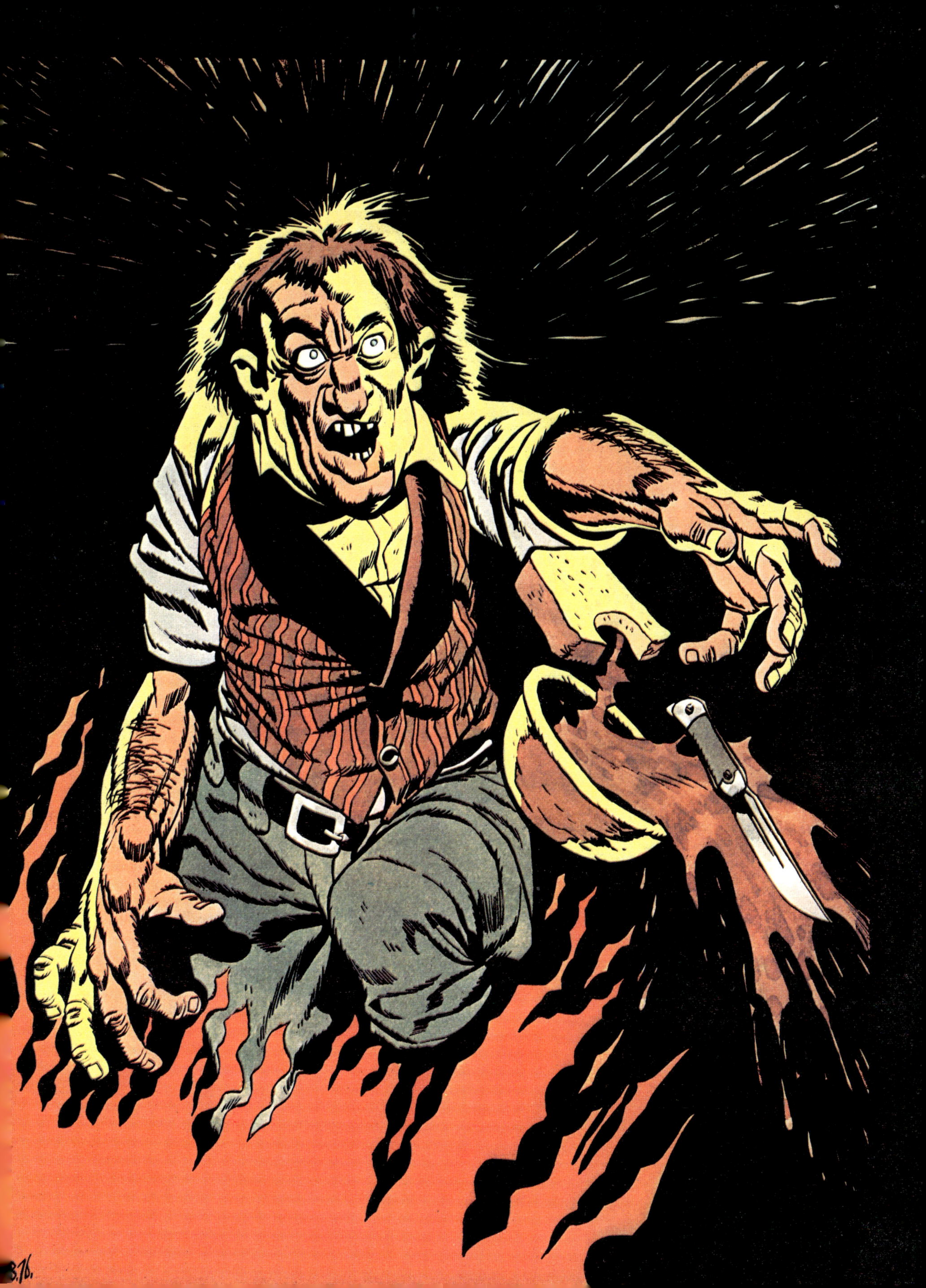

Some children inside screamed and a woman fainted on seeing me. The whole village was roused and the inhabitants were joined by some soldiers who had stopped at the inn. They pursued me out into the open country, throwing stones and attacking me with sticks. The soldiers fired their muskets as I ran across the fields and into the woods. I was afraid and tried to hide. Still they came after me and I heard shouts of 'devil' and 'daemon', which I did not then understand. I crouched beneath the roots of an old, old tree whilst all around me men and dogs trampled through the undergrowth. By now it was dark and they lit torches by which to see. To escape, I climbed up into

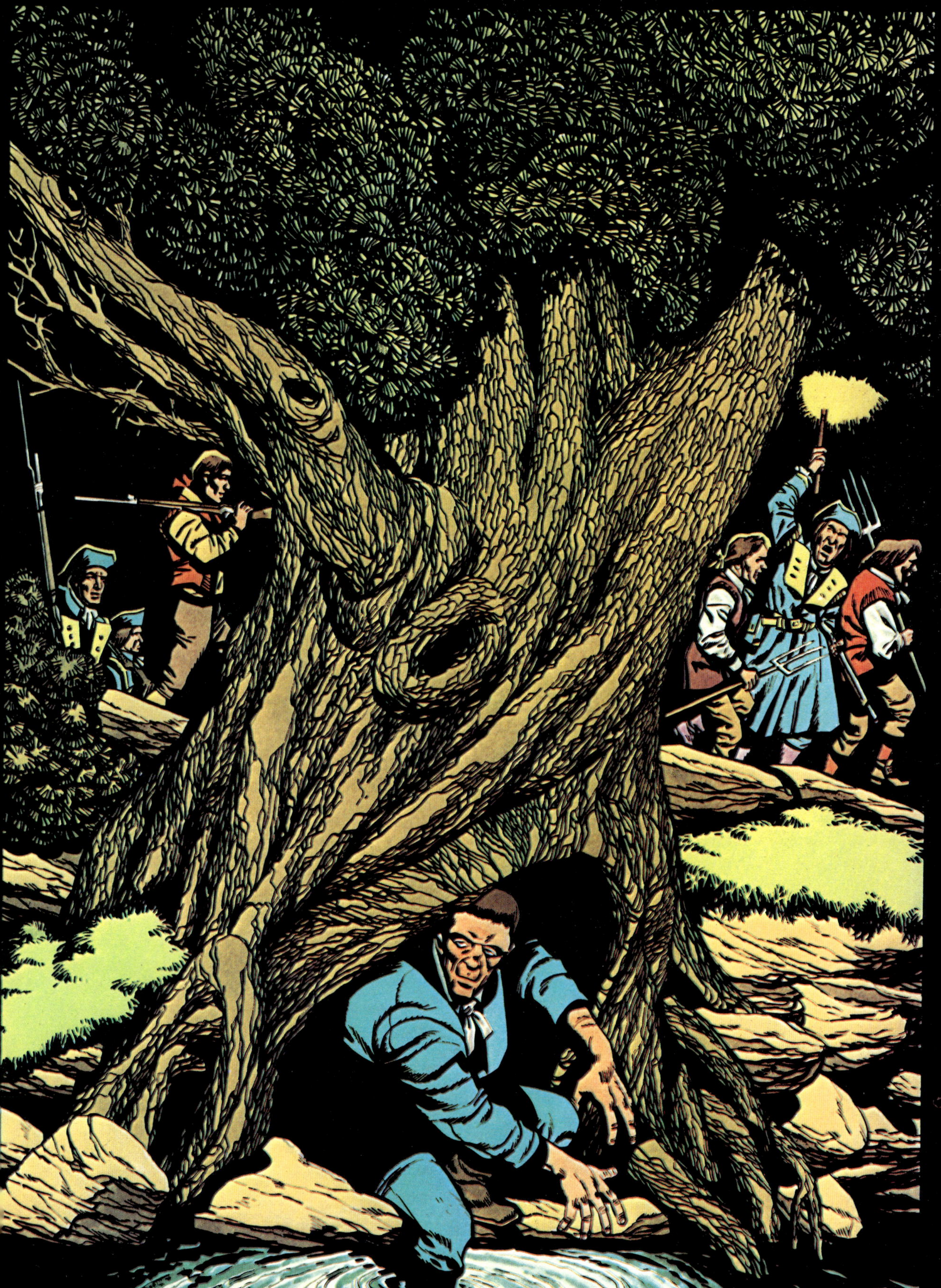

TABVLA TIPVM PACT
Thorough though my thoughts may have been I can only say the following:
MOTIVE POWER FORMAL MECHANICS IN THE USE OF GALVANISING EFFORTS USING ELECTRICAL FORCE

the tree and stayed there, motionless, until the commotion died away. I was afraid and remained in the tree all night to make sure I was no longer being hunted.

When dawn came, I climbed down and walked further into the forest until I came again to more open lands. I saw a neat cottage but I dared not go into it in case I was attacked; instead, I crept into a low wooden hut which leant against a wall of the building. It was dry but the many chinks in the wood let in the wind. The floor was of earth so I covered it with clean straw from a nearby pig-sty. I found that I was able to see into the cottage as the hut in which I sat enclosed a boarded up window and I could peer through the gaps between the planks.

There were three people living in the cottage: a young man and woman and an old man who was blind. The young man spent all day working out of doors while the young woman was busy inside their home. They showed great love and respect towards the old man, paying him every possible attention. I also saw that they were unhappy for sometimes the young man and woman appeared to weep. They were also very poor, with only the vegetables from their garden and the milk of one cow to live on. I decided not to steal food from them and help them by collecting firewood at night and leaving it outside their door.

Slowly, I began to realise that the sounds they made meant something to each other. Sometimes the sounds made them smile, sometimes they made them sad. I was very anxious to find out how this was done and so I applied myself to learning the system. As the winter progressed I learnt that the young man was called Felix and that the young woman was called Agatha. The old man they called 'father' and Agatha and Felix called each other 'sister' and 'brother'.

I noticed, too, that sometimes Felix read to the old man and Agatha. This puzzled me at first but then I decided that he found on the paper signs for speech which he understood. Of course, I could not hope to learn this science until I had mastered their language. And I knew I would have to do this before I dared reveal myself to them. It was about this time that, having admired the grace and beauty of the cottagers, I viewed myself in a clear pool and was horrified by what I saw. At first I could not believe it was I, but when I was convinced that I was the monster that I am, I was filled with bitter despondency.

As spring came, the old man walked outside occasionally, leaning on his son. New plants sprang up in the garden and life became less hard for them. One day, early in the summer, the lives of my friends—for that is how I thought of them—changed suddenly when a strange lady arrived on horseback. Felix was overcome with joy when he saw her and every trace of sorrow vanished from his face. His eyes sparkled, his cheek was flushed with pleasure. She was very beautiful but she did not make the same sounds as the family. They did not understand her and she did not understand them, so they made signs instead. Her name was Safie and both Agatha and her father were as pleased that she had come as Felix had been.

The days passed peacefully as before, except that there was joy where before there had only been sadness. I continued to learn their language and also gained some knowledge of the science of letters as Felix taught Safie using a book called *RUINS OF EMPIRES*. I obtained a basic knowledge of history in this way and found that man could be powerful and virtuous as well as vicious and cruel.

The more I heard about the way men lived, the more I realised the wretchedness of my own position. I was absolutely ignorant of my creator and had no money, no friends and no property. I was, as well, endowed with a deformed and loathsome body and not of the same nature as man. I was more agile and could live on a coarser diet; I could bear extremes of heat and cold more easily and my stature was greater than theirs. Was I then a monster, from which everyone fled and whom everyone disowned? I had no mother and no father; or if I had, then all memory of them had gone as I could only remember ever being as I was.

Soon after this I learned the full history of the family whom I watched. Their name was De Lacey and they came from France where they had once been affluent and successful. Felix had been upset when a Turkish mer-

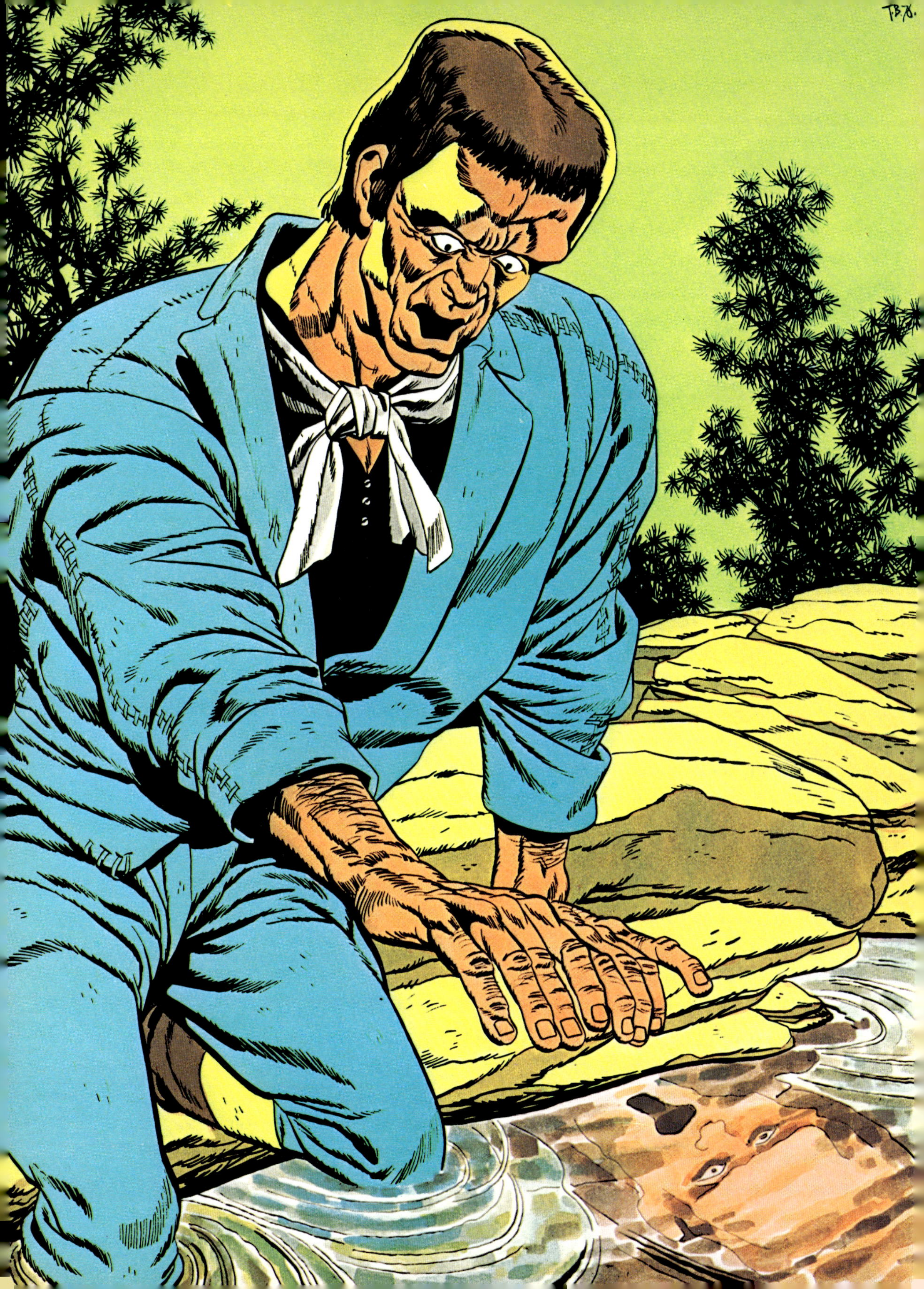

chant was condemned to death by the Government, because he thought that the man was innocent and so he decided to rescue him. Safie was the merchant's daughter and when he saw that Felix was attracted to her, the Turk said that Felix could marry her if the escape was successful. When the Government discovered that the merchant had escaped and that Felix had helped him, they threw old De Lacey and Agatha into prison. Felix returned from Italy, where he had taken the Turk, and surrendered to the law, hoping to free Agatha and his father by doing this. He failed and after five months in prison they were banished from their native country and went to live in the cottage in Germany where I found them. Safie's father had, in fact, no intention of letting her marry Felix but when Safie discovered what had happened to Felix she ran away and eventually found him.

I had discovered some papers in the pocket of the coat which I had taken from your room and now that I was able to read them I found that they were your journal covering the four months preceding my creation. The whole series of disgusting circumstances leading to my accursed origin was described, along with details of my odious and loathsome person. Why did you form a monster so hideous that even *you* turned from me in disgust? These were the reflections of my hours of despondency but when I contemplated the virtues of the cottagers I was sure that, when they were acquainted with my admiration of them, they would overlook my personal deformity.

As winter approached I decided that it was now time to introduce myself to the family. I resolved to enter the cottage when the old man was alone because, as he was blind, he would not be frightened by my appearance. One day, Safie, Agatha and Felix went on a country walk. All was silent around the cottage: it was an excellent opportunity. I approached the door of the cottage and knocked.

'Who is there?' said the old man. 'Come in.'

'Pardon this intrusion,' I said. 'I am a traveller in want of a little rest. I would be grateful if I could remain before the fire for a few minutes.'

'Enter,' said De Lacey. 'I will try to relieve your wants but my children are out and, as I am blind, I will not be able to bring you any food.'

'Do not trouble yourself. It is only warmth and rest that I need. I am on my way to claim the protection of some friends, whom I sincerely love, and who I hope will treat me favourably. I am an unfortunate and deserted creature with no friend or relation upon earth. These people I am going to have never seen me and I am afraid, for if I fail, I am an outcast in the world for ever.'

'Do not despair,' De Lacey said. 'The hearts of men are full of brotherly love and charity. If these friends are good and amiable all will be well.'

'They are kind,' I said, 'but they are prejudiced against me and where they ought to see a friend they see only a detestable monster.'

'Where do these friends reside?'

'Near this spot.'

'May I know the names and residence of your friends?' he asked.

I paused. This was the moment of decision. I struggled vainly to answer him but I could only sink to the floor, sobbing. At that moment I heard the footsteps of the others approaching. I had not a moment to lose and I seized De Lacey's hand.

'Now is the time!' I cried. 'Save and protect me! You and your family are the friends I seek. Do not desert me in my hour of trial!'

'Great God!' exclaimed the old man. 'Who are you?'

At that moment the cottage door opened and Felix, Safie and Agatha came in. Who can describe their horror and consternation on seeing me? Agatha fainted, Safie rushed out of the cottage and Felix darted forward, tearing me from his father's knees. He dashed me to the ground and struck me violently with a stick. I could have torn him limb from limb but my heart sank within me; overcome by pain and anguish I quit the cottage and escaped to my hovel.

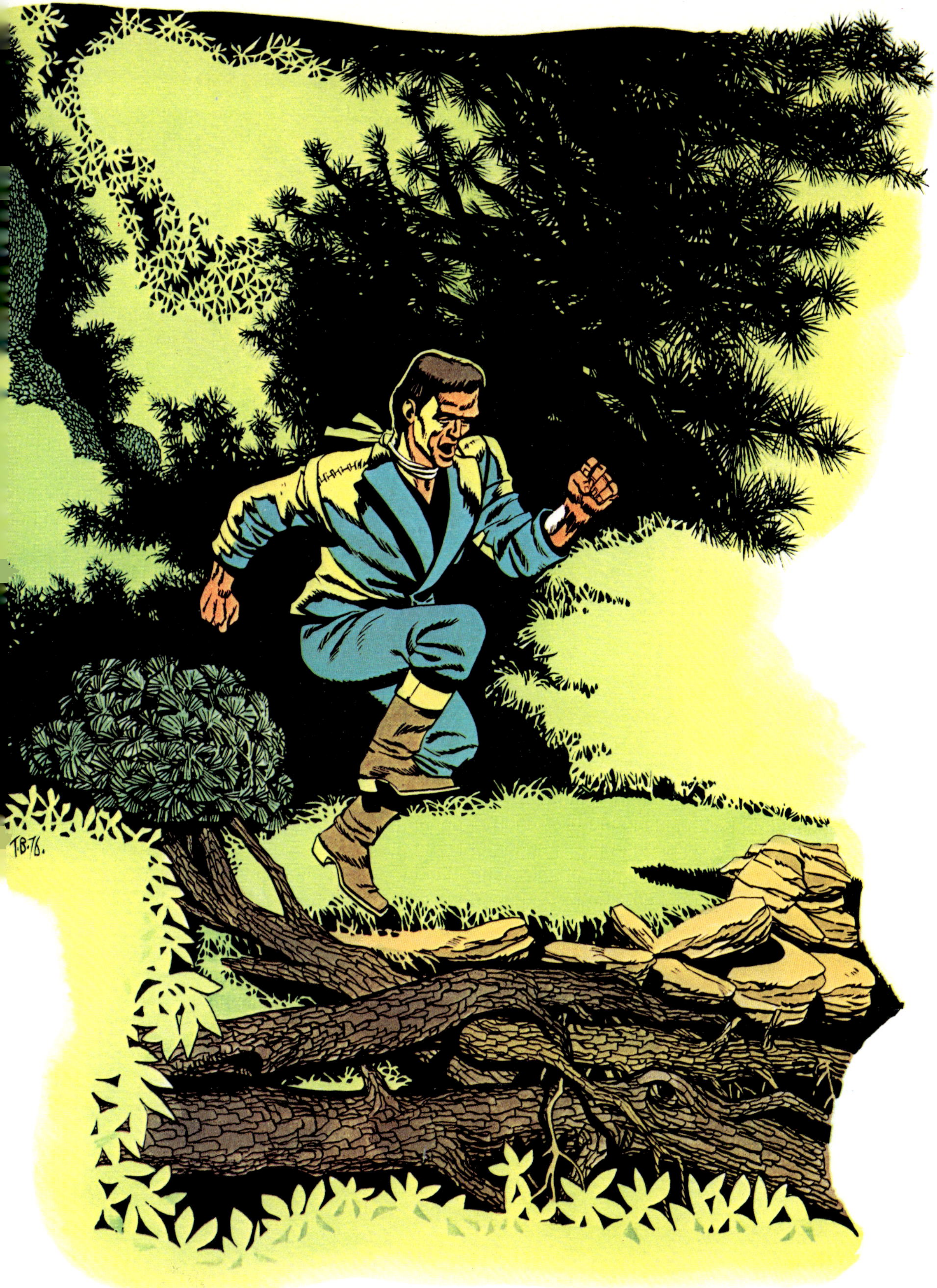
T.B.76.

My feelings were of rage and revenge. I could have gladly destroyed the cottage and its inhabitants, glutting myself with their shrieks and misery. That night I wandered in the woods, howling in anguish. As the sun rose, the pleasantness of the day restored to me some degree of tranquillity. I decided that I had acted imprudently by allowing De Lacey's children to see me. Far better to have made friends with the old man first and then, little by little, introduce myself to the rest of the family. I stayed in the wood for the rest of the day, returning to the cottage at night. But next morning I realised that the place was empty: the family had gone. Then Felix approached with another man and it was clear from their conversation that the De Laceys were leaving.

'My father's life is in the greatest danger,' said Felix. 'Take possession of your cottage and let me fly from this awful place.'

I spent the rest of the day in a state of utter despair. The feelings of revenge and hatred which welled up inside me could not be contained. At night, I placed wood and straw around the cottage and, having destroyed every trace of cultivation in the garden, I set light to it and danced with fury around the cottage as it burned. As soon as I was certain that no-one could save the building, I took refuge in the woods.

I resolved to leave the scene of my misfortunes and look for you. I knew from your papers that Geneva was your native town so I set off on a long and difficult journey, travelling usually only by night in case I should be

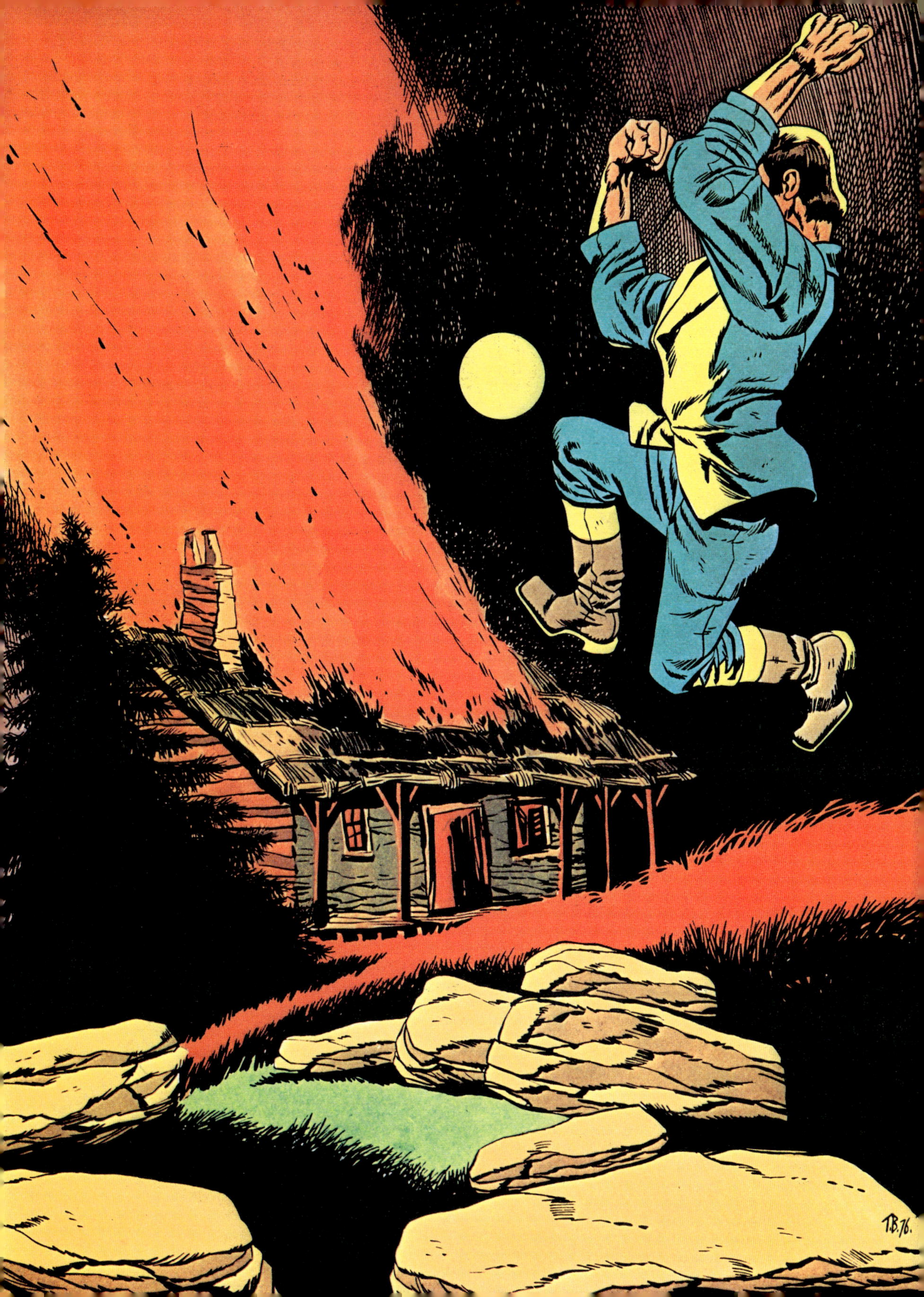

seen. One morning, finding that my path lay through a deep wood, I ventured to continue my journey after the sun had risen. I came to a river and, not knowing which way to go next, I paused a while. Hearing voices, I concealed myself beneath a cypress tree. A young girl came running along the river bank and, as she neared me, she slipped and fell in. I rushed from my hiding place and, fighting against the force of the current, saved her and dragged her to the shore. She showed no sign of life and I was trying to revive her when a rustic approached. He tore the girl from my arms and hurried into the wood. I followed him—I know not why—and when he saw me, he aimed his gun at me and fired. I sank to the ground, injured in the shoulder.

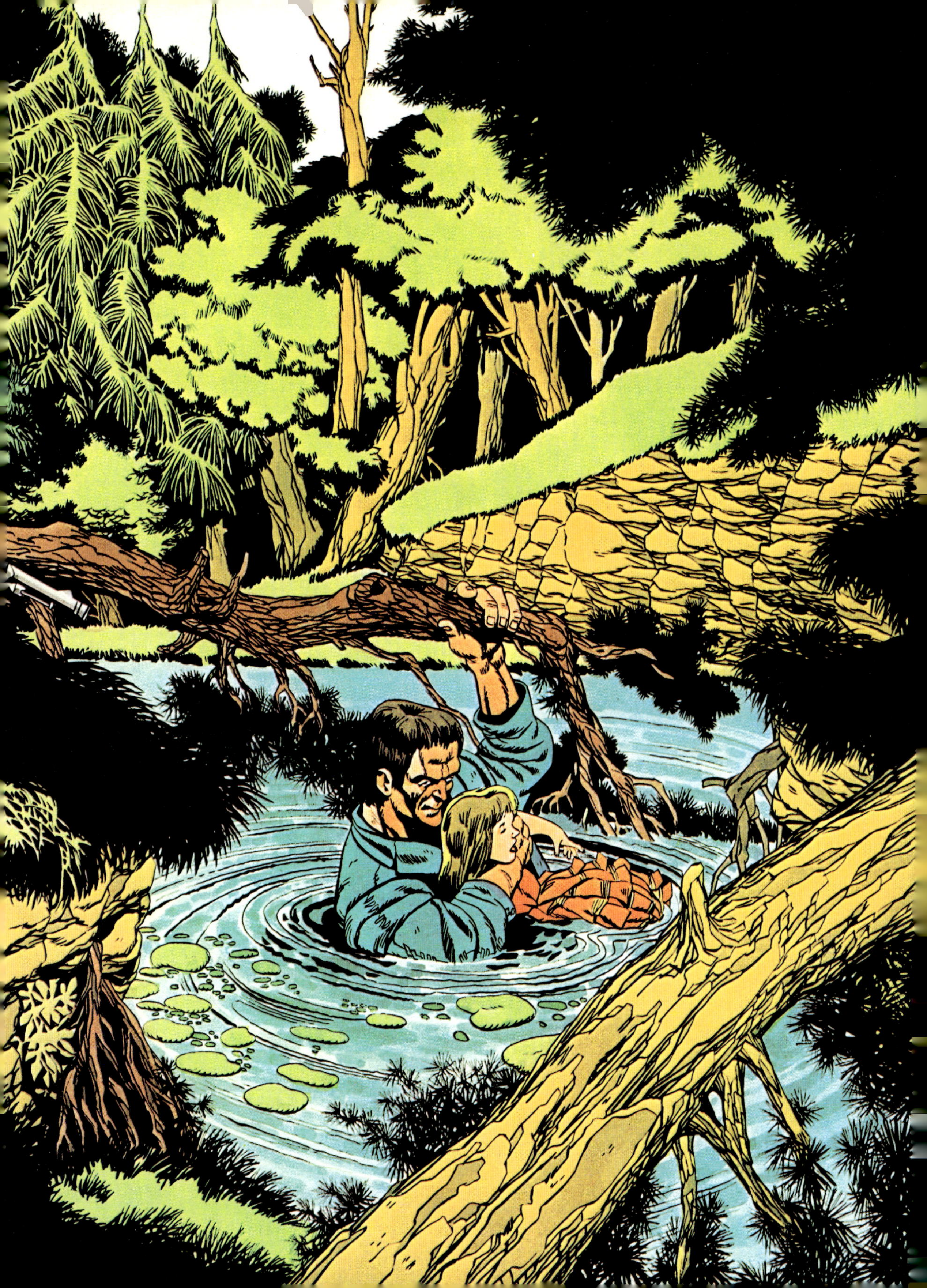

This, then, was the reward for my benevolence! I had saved a human being from death and, as a reward, I writhed under the miserable hurt of a wound. Inflamed by pain, I vowed eternal hatred and vengeance to all mankind. For some weeks I led an unhappy life in the woods, trying to cure the wound which did, at last, heal. I continued my journey and two months later reached the outskirts of Geneva.

It was evening when I arrived and, as usual, I found a hiding place in the fields, whilst deciding how to approach you. I was disturbed by a beautiful child who came running into the recess I had chosen. Suddenly an idea seized me: this little creature had lived too short a time to be afraid of deformity. I would seize him and educate him as my companion and friend. I grabbed him as he passed and drew him towards me. As soon as he beheld my form he screamed.

'What is the meaning of this?' I said, 'I do not wish to hurt you.'

He struggled violently, crying: 'Let me go, monster! You wish to tear me to pieces. Let me go or I will tell my papa. He is a judge, he is Mr Frankenstein—he will punish you!'

'Frankenstein!' I cried. 'You belong to my enemy towards whom I have sworn revenge. You shall be my first victim.'

The child still struggled, calling me an ogre, an ugly wretch. I grasped his throat to silence him and in a moment he lay dead at my feet. My heart swelled with triumph. My enemy was not invulnerable! I, too, could create misery and despair. As I looked at the child, I saw something glittering on his chest. It was a portrait of a lovely woman and, for a moment, I gazed with delight on her beautiful face. Then I remembered that I was for ever deprived of the pleasures such creatures could bestow. Overcome by feelings of hatred for all humans, I sought a secluded hiding place. I entered a barn in which a young woman was sleeping on some straw. Another whose favours I would never receive! Thanks to the lessons of Felix I had learnt to work mischief so I placed the portrait securely in a fold of her dress and fled.

At length, I wandered towards these mountains, con-

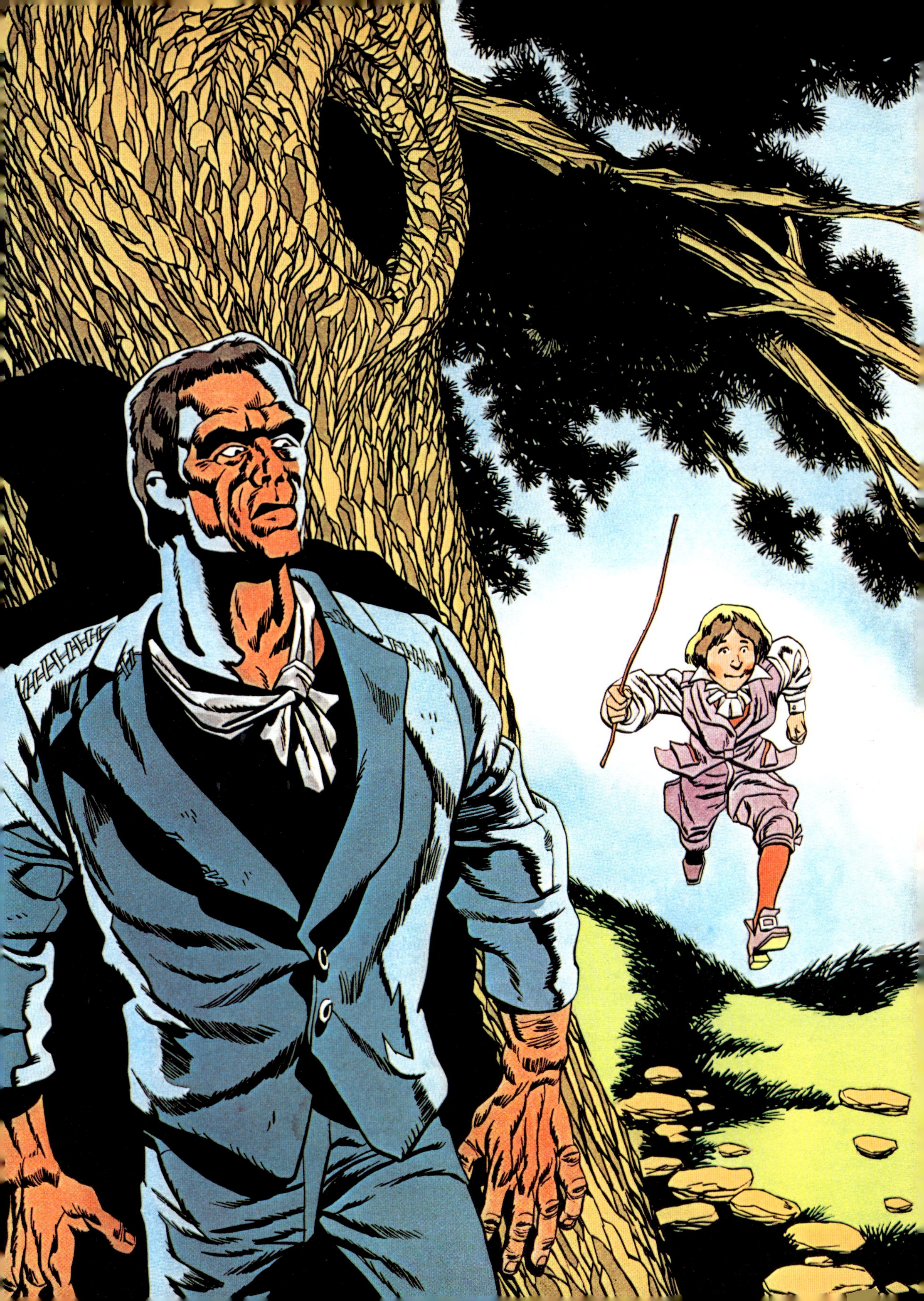

sumed by a burning passion which you alone can gratify. We shall not part until you have promised to comply with my request. I am alone and miserable. Man will not associate with me but one as deformed and horrible as myself would not deny me. My companion must be of the same species and have the same defects. You must make for me a wife.

CHAPTER FOUR

Victor Frankenstein's Story

I WAS bewildered, perplexed and could not fully comprehend his meaning.

'I demand this female creature of you as right,' he continued, 'a right which you must not refuse.'

'I do refuse it,' I replied' 'and no torture shall drag consent from me. I cannot create another like you whose joint wickedness might desolate the world.'

'Have a care,' the daemon declared, 'for I will work at your destruction so that you shall curse the hour of your birth.'

A fiendish rage animated him as he said this, his face wrinkled into horrible contortions. Presently, he calmed himself and continued.

'What I ask of you is reasonable and moderate. I demand a creature of another sex but as hideous as myself. We shall, it is true, be monsters, cut off from the world. Our lives will not be happy but they will be harmless. Oh! My creator, let me see that I excite the sympathy of some living thing.'

I was moved and I felt that there was some justice in his argument. His tale and the feelings he expressed proved him to be a creature of fine sensations. But still I doubted the wisdom of granting his request.

'You swear,' I said, 'to be harmless and yet you have already shown a degree of malice that makes me distrust you.'

'If I have no ties and no affections, hatred and vice must be my lot. The love of another will destroy the cause of my crimes: I shall become linked to the chain of existence and events from which I am now shut out.'

After reflecting carefully for some minutes, I decided that the justice due to him and my fellow creatures compelled me to comply with his request.

'I consent to your demand, on your solemn oath to leave Europe for ever and keep away from every place close to man as soon as I deliver to you a female who will share your exile.'

'I swear!' he cried, 'by the sun and by the blue sky of

Heaven and by the fire of love that burns in my heart. Go and start your work. I shall watch your progress and when you are ready I shall appear.'

So saying, he ran from the hut, rapidly descended the mountain and was quickly lost to sight amid the undulations of the ice. It was nearly the end of the day and I began my journey back to Chamounix. Night was far advanced when I came to the half-way resting place. The stars shone at intervals as the clouds passed before them and the dark pines rose before me. It was a scene of wonderful solemnity and stirred strange thoughts within me. I wept bitterly.

'Oh! Stars and clouds and winds, you are all about to mock me. If you really pity me, crush sensation and memory, let me become as nothing. But if not, depart and leave me in darkness.'

After returning to Geneva I found that I could not bring myself to recommence my work. I feared the vengeance of the disappointed fiend, yet I was unable to overcome my repugnance for the work which I had promised to do. I had heard that some discoveries had been made by English scientists which would help me. I decided, therefore, to go to London and meet them. Before I left, however, my father talked with me about Elizabeth.

'I have always looked forward to your marriage with our dear Elizabeth but you, perhaps, regard her as your sister and do not wish her to become your wife. You may have met another whom you love and this conflict of emotions may be the cause of the misery which you feel.'

'My dear father, be re-assured. I love Elizabeth tenderly and sincerely. My future hopes and prospects are entirely bound up in the expectation of our marriage.'

My father then asked me if I had any objection to the marriage taking place very soon. How could I agree? I was bound by a solemn promise which I had not yet fulfilled and of which I dare not speak. I must perform my task and let the monster depart before taking Elizabeth as my wife. I remembered also that I must go to England before commencing the creation of a female being. So I told my father that, before I was wed, I wished to pay a visit to England to completely restore my spirits. He agreed that I should go but asked that I should not stay more than a year.

It was towards the end of September that I left my country once again. My father, unknown to me, had arranged for Henry Clerval to join me at Strasbourg. Although this interfered with the solitude I needed for my task, it was pleasant to have a companion. I was afraid of one thing—that, during my absence, my family would be at the mercy of the daemon. But I recalled that he said he would follow me and I soothed my fears with this thought.

London was our first port of call and we planned to stay some weeks in this wonderful and celebrated city where I quickly acquainted myself with the most distinguished natural philosophers of the day. I had received a letter from a friend in Scotland who invited us to visit him in Perth. Clerval said he wished to see Scotland but would also like to see more of England first so, as I was anxious to begin my work, we agreed that I would proceed immediately to Scotland while he visited Windsor, Oxford and other historic places. We would then meet again in Perth in the summer, for it was now March.

When I arrived at Perth I remained but a few days with my friend, explaining that I wished to tour the remoter parts of north Scotland. I decided after some exploration that a remote island in the Orkneys would best suit my dark purpose. It was hardly more than a rock whose high sides were continually beaten by the waves. Its inhabitants consisted of but five persons and a few cows. I hired a mean, two-roomed cottage for my stay. Its walls were unplastered, the thatch was in poor condition but it served me well enough. In this retreat I devoted the mornings to my work and in the afternoons I walked on the stony beach, listening to the waves as they roared at my feet. At times I could not bring myself to continue with my filthy and loathsome task for several days. On other occasions, I toiled day and night in order to complete the creature.

One evening as I sat in my laboratory, a train of reflection occurred to me which led me to consider the effects of what I was now doing. Suppose the creature I was now making became ten thousand times more malignant than her mate? He had sworn to keep away from man, but she had not. They might even hate each other for if he loathed his own appearance might he not detest it when it came before his eyes in female form? Even if they did inhabit the deserts of the world, they might still have children and propagate a race of daemons who would terrorise men. For the first time the wickedness of my promise burst upon me. I shuddered to think that future generations might curse my name. I trembled and my heart failed within me; when I looked up I saw, by the light of the moon, the daemon at the window. A ghastly grin wrinkled his lips as he gazed upon me where I sat fulfilling the task which he had allotted to me. As I looked on him, his countenance expressed the utmost malice and treachery. I thought with a sensation of madness of my promise to create another like him and, shaking with passion, I tore to pieces the thing on which I was

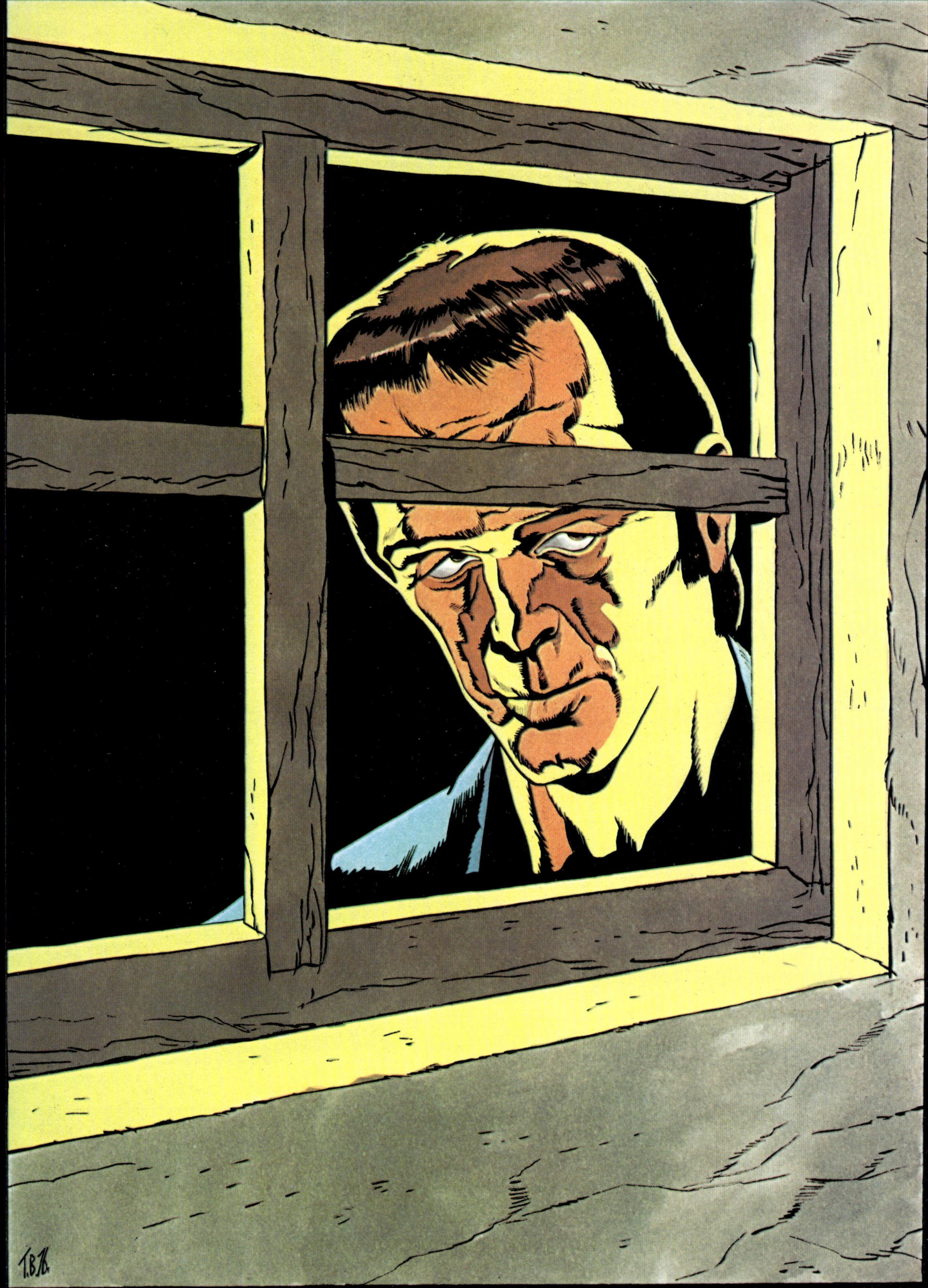
T.B.76.

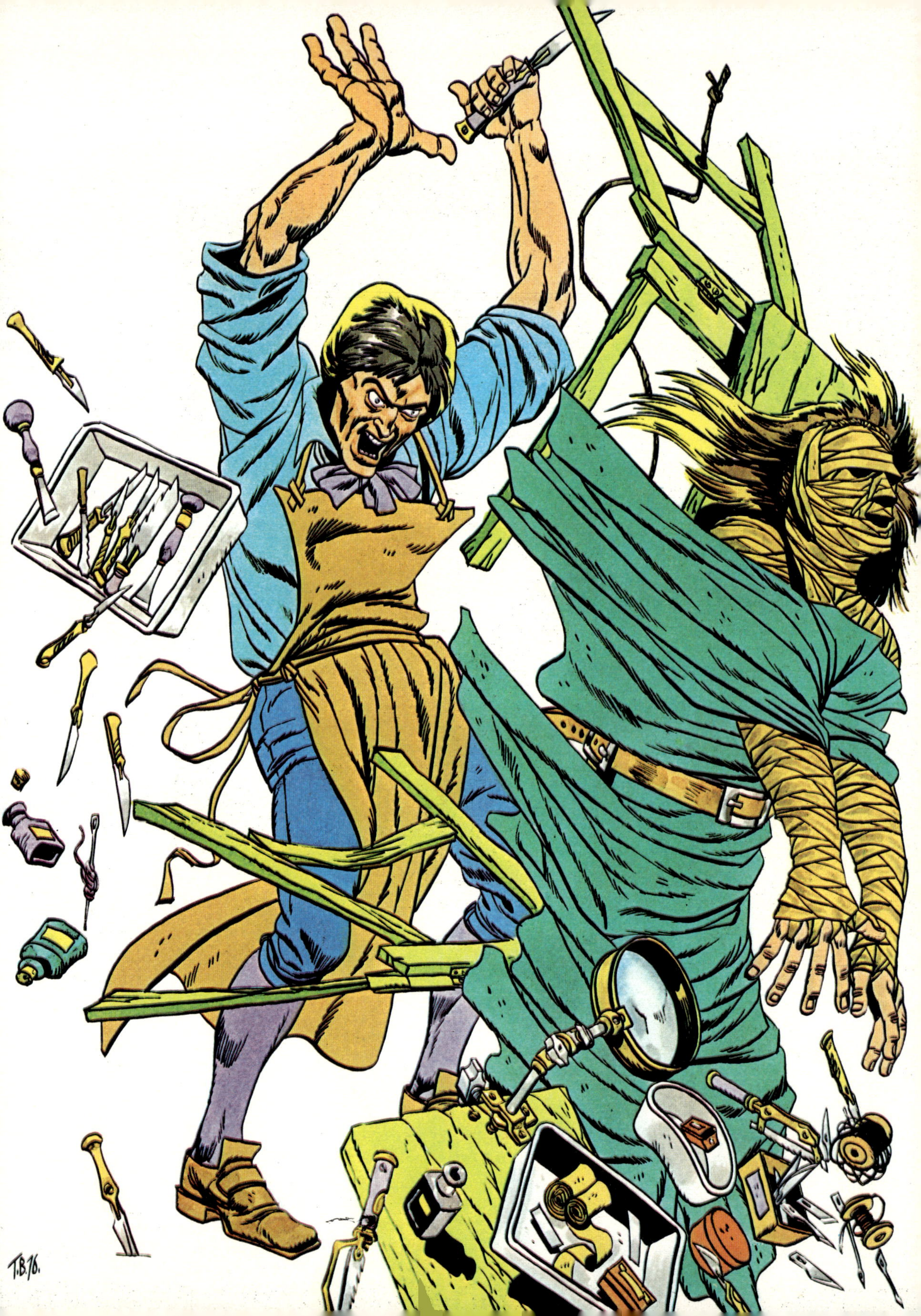
T.B.76.

engaged. I heard the creaking of my door and footsteps in the passage: the creature entered my laboratory. Speaking in a smothered voice, he said:

'You have destroyed the work which you began. Do you dare break your promise? I have endured toil and misery, following you to England, dwelling in the deserts of Scotland. Untold fatigue, cold and hunger have been my lot and yet you dare destroy my hopes?'

'Never again will I create another like yourself, equal in deformity and wickedness.'

'Remember,' he said, a fierce passion informing his words, 'that I can make the very light of day painful to you. You are my creator but I am your master. You will obey.'

'Your threats cannot move me to such a wicked act. Begone! I am firm and your words will only increase my rage.'

The monster gnashed his teeth in impotent fury.

'Shall each man find a wife for himself and shall I be alone? Are you to be happy while I am wretched? You may blast my other passions but revenge remains. Beware, for I am fearless and therefore powerful. Frankenstein, you will repent of the injuries with which you wound my soul. I go—but remember, I shall be with you on your wedding night.'

I would have seized him but he evaded me and rapidly left the house. A few moments later I saw him in his boat which was soon lost among the waves.

✱ ✱ ✱ ✱

The night passed away and, as the sun rose, my feelings became calmer. But I still despaired as I recalled his last words. In that hour I should die, to satisfy and extinguish his malice. Beloved Elizabeth! How she would weep when her lover was so barbarously snatched from her. Tears streamed from my eyes and I resolved not to fall without a bitter struggle. I decided to leave the island and return to Perth, to meet up again with Henry Clerval. But, before I set out, there was a task to perform. I must pack up my chemical instruments and dispose of the remnants which were to have been the daemon's mate. I put the pieces of flesh and limbs into a basket weighted with stones, determining to throw them into the sea. I waited until it was quite dark and when the moon rose I sailed out about four miles in a little skiff and cast the basket into the sea. The air, though chill, was pure and the agreeable sensations which filled me led me to stay longer on the water and, fixing the rudder, I stretched out in the bottom of the boat.

When I awoke, I found the sun well up in the sky and a strong wind blowing. I could only sail before the wind, not knowing where I was going. As the sun descended towards the horizon, I spied land towards the south and steered towards this sanctuary. As I neared the coast, I saw a little town and a good harbour. As I tied my boat up, a crowd of people approached, whispering together. I heard that they spoke English so, addressing them in that language, I asked them what town this was.

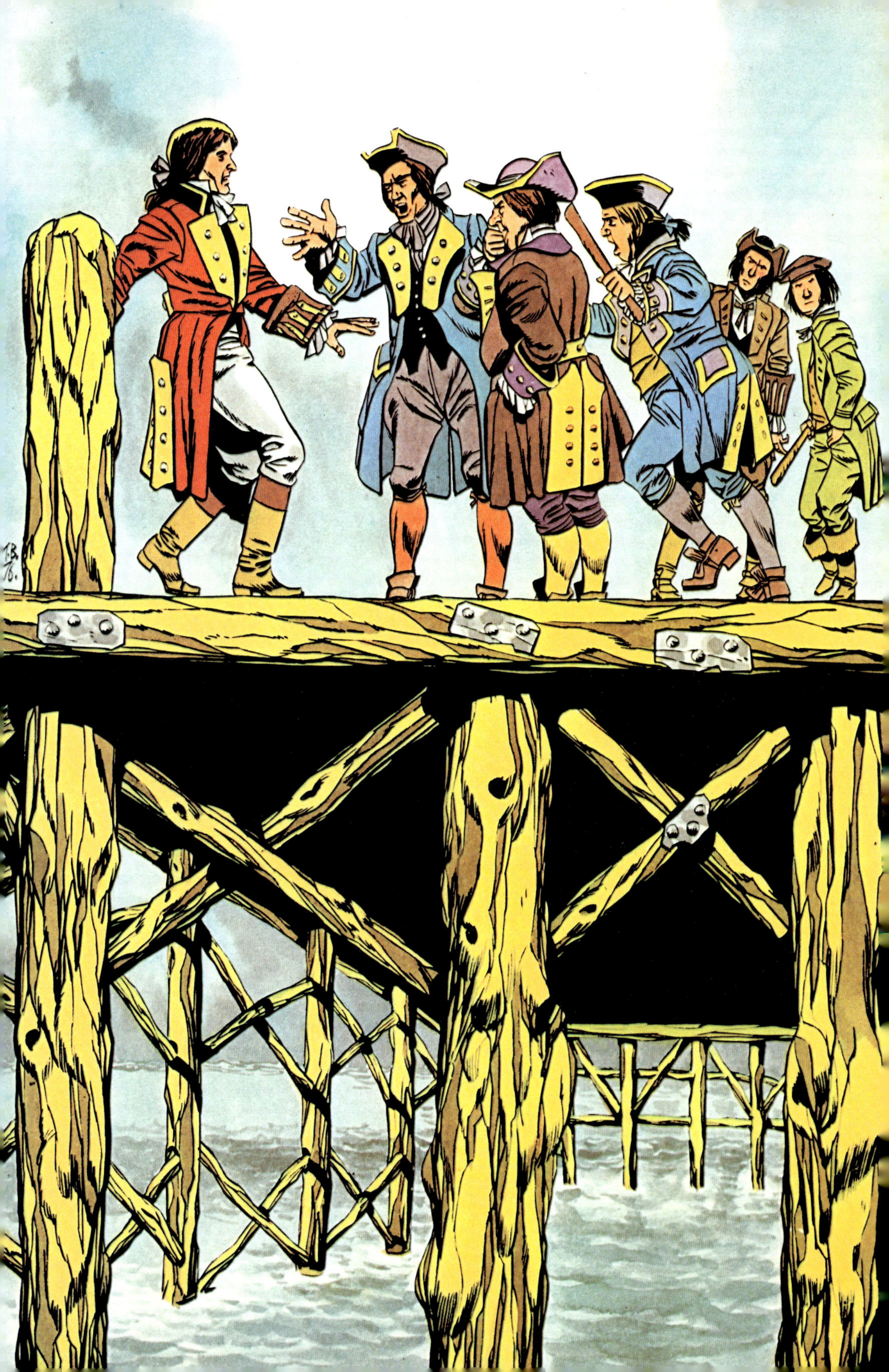

'You will know soon enough,' replied a man with a hoarse voice. 'Maybe you are come to a place that will not prove much to your taste, but you will not be consulted as to your quarters, I promise you.'

I was surprised at the rudeness of his answer, and disconcerted by the angry faces of his companions. I remarked that it was not usually the custom of Englishmen to receive strangers so inhospitably.

'I do not know,' said the man, 'what the custom of the English may be but it is the custom of the Irish to hate villains. Come, sir, you must follow me to Mr Kirwin's house and give an account of yourself.'

Upon enquiry, I learnt that Mr Kirwin was a magistrate and that I was to give an account of the death of a gentleman who had been found murdered the previous night.

Mr Kirwin was an old, benevolent man with calm and mild manners, although he looked upon me with some severity. One of the men who had accompanied me to his house described how he and his son and brother-in-law had discovered the body of a man on the beach of a nearby creek. They thought he had been drowned but found that his clothes were dry and he had, apparently, been strangled, for there were black marks of fingers on his neck. I recalled the marks found on William's neck and became agitated. The magistrate noted my condition, and drew an unfavourable conclusion from it.

Another man swore that, just before the corpse was found, he had seen a boat with one man in it not far from the shore. As far as he could judge, it was the same boat in which I had just landed.

Following this evidence, Mr Kirwin ordered that I should be taken to the room in which the body lay to observe the effect which seeing it would produce. I entered the room and went up to the coffin. How can I describe my sensations on beholding the corpse? I felt parched with horror and gasped for breath. The events of the day passed like a dream from my memory when I saw, stretched before me, the lifeless form of Henry Clerval.

✻ ✻ ✻ ✻

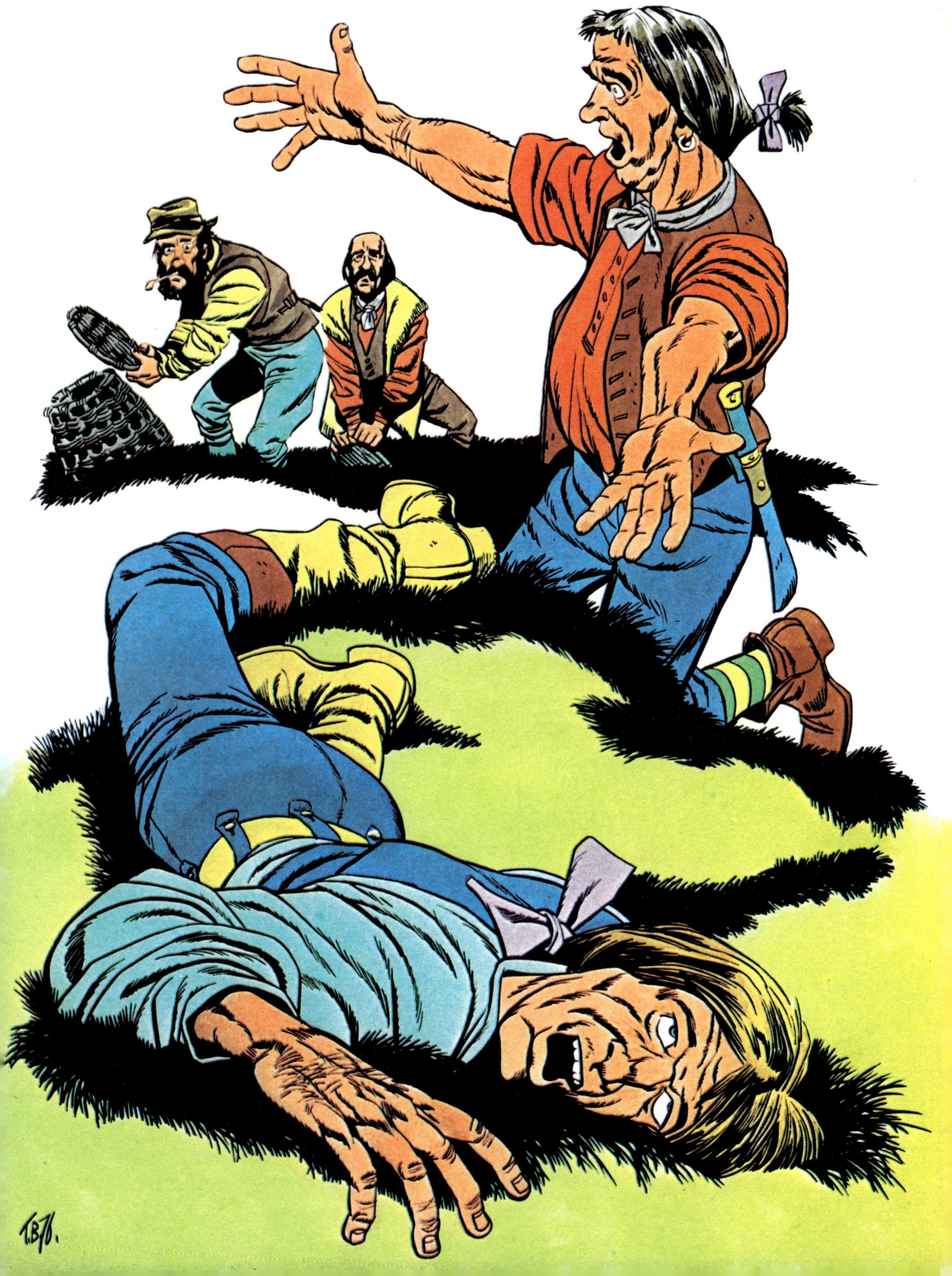

The human frame could no longer support the agonies I endured and I was carried out of the room crying:

'Two I have already destroyed, but you, my friend Clerval, my benefactor. Have my murderous machinations deprived you, my dearest Henry, of life?'

A nervous fever followed this collapse and, for many weeks, I lay close to death, raving in a frightful way. Slowly, I recovered control of my mind to find myself in a prison cell, watched by an old nurse. I learnt that Mr Kirwin had provided both her and a physician to tend me during my illness.

I was overcome by gloom and misery, and wished that I was dead rather than alive in a world so replete with wretchedness. I even considered confessing my guilt and suffering the penalty of the law. Such were my thoughts when Mr Kirwin came into my room. He said that he was sure that evidence could be brought to clear me from the charge of murder.

'Immediately upon your being taken ill,' he explained, 'all your papers were brought to me and I discovered a letter from your father. I instantly wrote to Geneva, and that was two months ago. Your family is perfectly well and someone, a friend, has come to visit you.'

He rose and left my room and, in a moment, my father entered. Nothing could have given me greater pleasure and I stretched out my hands to him.

'Are you then safe? And Elizabeth, and Ernest?'

He calmed me with assurances of their welfare and tried to raise my spirits with news of them. We were not allowed to talk for long as Mr Kirwin did not want me exhausted. After another four weeks had passed, the assizes were held at which my case was presented. Mr Kirwin collected witnesses and arranged for my defence and it was proved that I was on the island in the Orkneys at the time Clerval's body was found.

I was set free and, although my father was afraid I was too weak to withstand the journey, I insisted on leaving Ireland. I was anxious to return to Geneva and watch over the lives of those I loved, and to lie in wait for the murderer. We went by sea to Le Havre and thence to Paris where we rested for a while. Eventually, we arrived at Geneva and Elizabeth welcomed me with warm

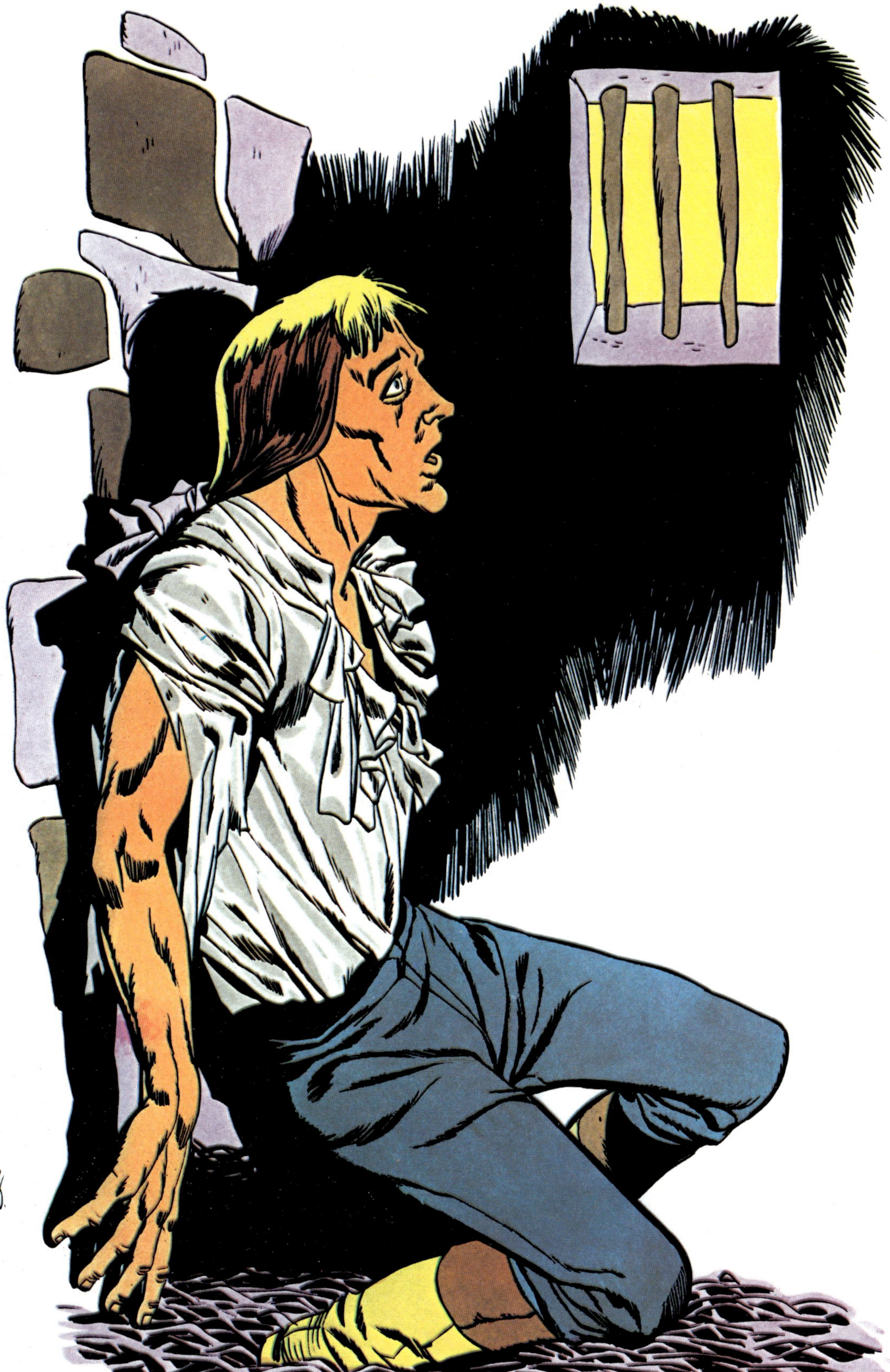

affection although she was clearly distressed by my emaciated frame.

Despite the tranquillity of life at Geneva, I continued to suffer fits of rage and despondency. Elizabeth alone had the power to draw me from these onslaughts; her gentle voice would soothe me. She wept with me and for me.

Soon after my arrival, my father spoke again of my marriage with Elizabeth. Despite my fears springing from the dread words of the creature, I agreed that the day should be fixed. I assumed, as best I could, a mantle of gaiety so that none, most particularly my sweet Elizabeth, should detect the apprehension with which I approached what should have been the most happy of days.

As preparations for the nuptials proceeded apace, I took every precaution to defend myself in case the fiend should openly attack me. I carried pistols and a dagger at all times, which gave me a greater feeling of security. Elizabeth seemed happy, and my calm manner soothed her mind. But on the day that was to fulfil my destiny, she was melancholy and pervaded by a presentiment of evil. I had promised to reveal my dreadful secret to her the day after our wedding, so perhaps she thought of this.

After the ceremony, a large party assembled at my father's house to bid us farewell as we began our journey to Lake Como, going first by boat to Evian where we would spend our wedding night.

'I shall be with you on your wedding night.'

The monster's words were ever with me as our boat glided along and we admired the grandeur of the scenery, with mountains all around and, in the distance, the beautiful Mont Blanc. As the sun sank lower in the heavens we perceived the spire of Evian, landing there at eight o'clock. We walked for a short while on the shore, enjoying the transitory light of dusk and then retired to the inn. The wind, which had fallen in the south, now rose with great violence in the west. Clouds swept across the moon and a heavy storm of rain descended. As soon as night fell, a thousand fears arose in my mind. Every sound terrified me but I resolved that I would sell my life dearly. Elizabeth observed my agitation and asked what troubled me.

'Peace, my love,' I said. 'This night, and all will be safe; but this night is dreadful, very dreadful.'

I entreated her to retire, having decided not to join her until I knew where my enemy was. I continued walking up and down the passages of the house, inspecting every corner where he might be hiding. But I discovered no trace of him and began to think that something had happened to prevent him carrying out his threat. Suddenly I heard a shrill and awful scream. It came from Elizabeth's room.

As I heard it, the truth dawned upon me and, momentarily, I could not move. The scream was repeated and I rushed into the room. I saw at the open window that most hideous and abhorred figure. A grin was on the monster's face and he seemed to jeer as he pointed towards the bed then leaped from the ledge. Elizabeth was there, lifeless and inanimate, thrown across the bed, her pale, distorted features half covered by her hair. The murderous mark of the fiend's grasp was on her neck.

✦ ✦ ✦ ✦

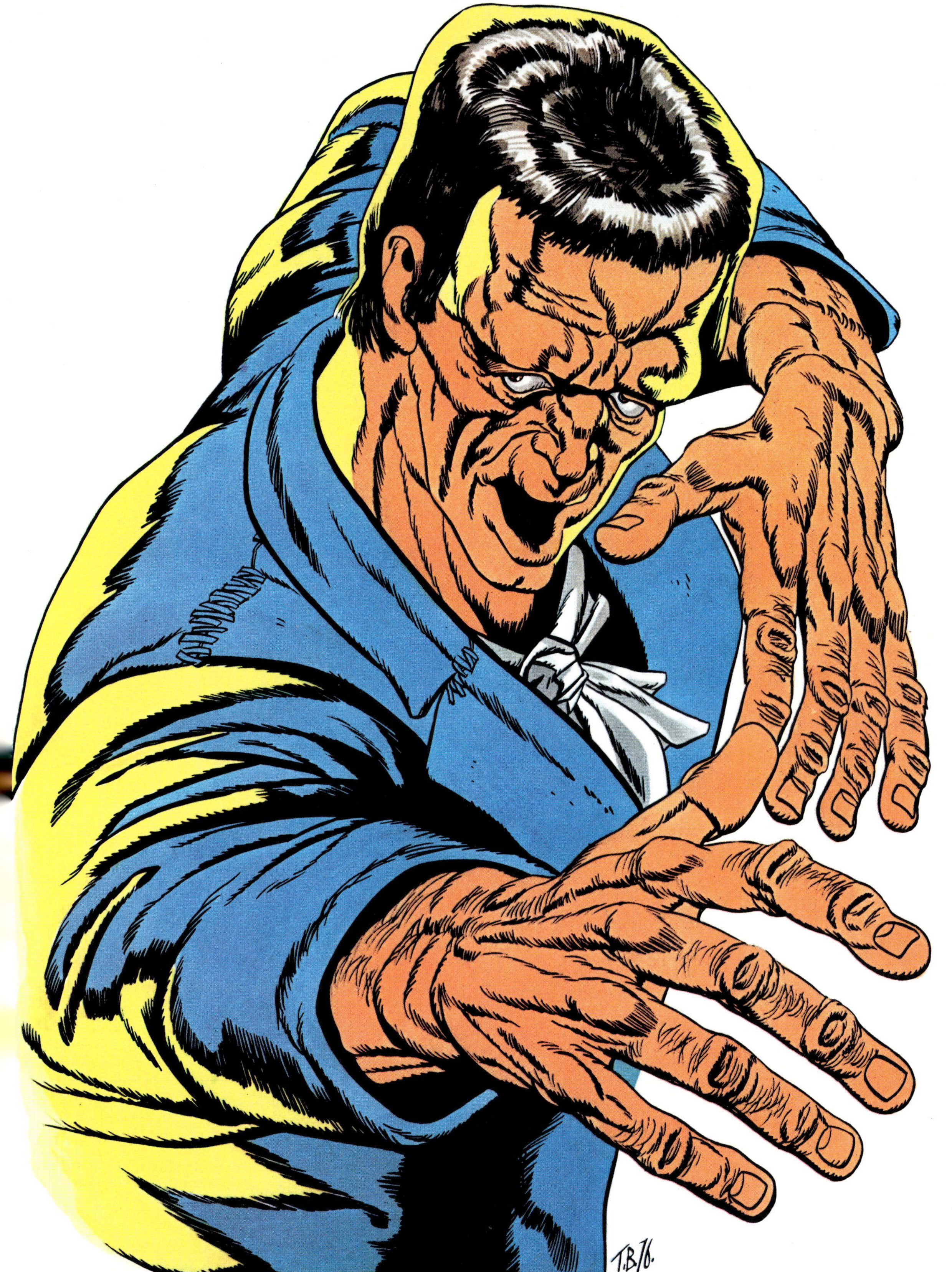
T.B/76.

In a mood of black despair, I engaged the assistance of people of the town to track down the creature but no trace of him could be found. I was bewildered, enveloped in a cloud of wonder and horror. The death of William, the execution of Justine, the murder of Clerval and now, the slaughter of my wife. Realising that my father and Ernest were both in danger, I set off for Geneva with all possible speed.

It was with relief that I found them both alive but my father sank under the tidings which I bore. His eyes wandered vacantly, having lost that which he held most dear. He could not live under the weight of the horrors that accumulated around him; the springs of existence gave way and in a few days he died in my arms.

    The body of my beloved had been brought from Evian and, with heavy hearts, Ernest and I prepared to lay her and my father to rest next to our cherished William. It was a sad procession which trudged to the cemetery that day behind the two coffins. Good friends of my father's, who had also known and loved Elizabeth, joined us in mourning their passing. As they were committed to the ground, the drab greyness of the day was accentuated as a soft rain pattered down. One by one the mourners left the churchyard and even Ernest, whose grief was as insupportable as my own, could no longer tarry by the graves

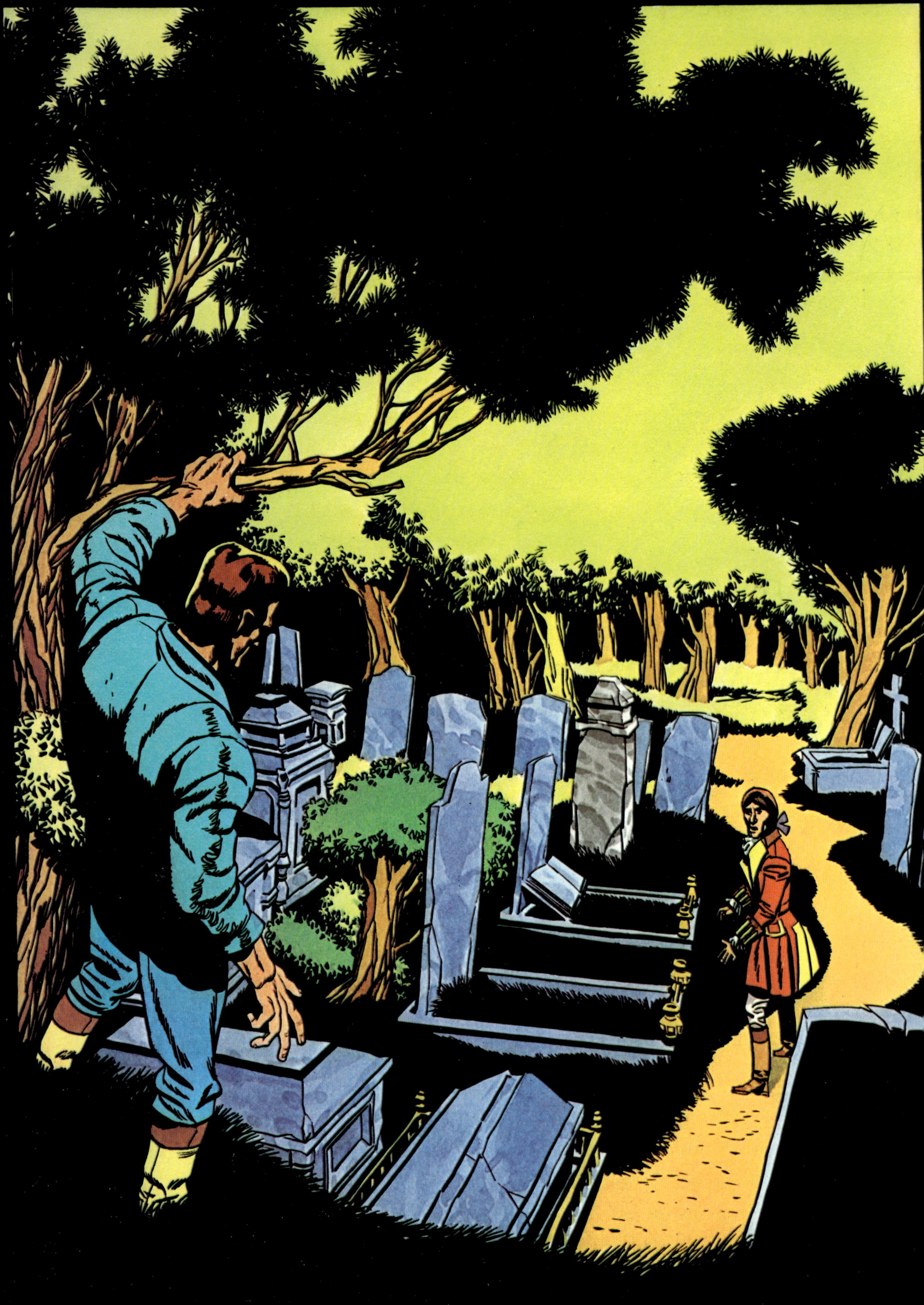

and returned to the empty house. Transfixed with sorrow, shaking with fury, I knelt by their graves and wept. All was silent, except the leaves of the trees which were gently agitated by the wind. It was nearly dark as I kissed the earth beneath which my father and my wife lay.

'By the sacred earth on which I kneel,' I cried, 'I swear by the spirits that preside over you, my loved ones, that I shall pursue the daemon who caused this misery until he or I shall perish in mortal conflict. Let the cursed and hellish monster drink deep in agony; let him feel the despair that now torments me.'

I was answered through the stillness of the night by a loud and fiendish laugh. It died away and a well-known and abhorrent voice addressed me in an audible whisper.

'I am satisfied, miserable wretch! You have determined to live and I am satisfied.'

I darted towards the spot from which the sound proceeded. Suddenly the broad disk of the moon rose and shone full upon his ghastly and distorted shape as he fled with more than mortal speed.

✻ ✻ ✻ ✻

I resolved to hunt the daemon to the death and, providing myself with a sum of money, together with a few of my mother's jewels, I departed. I experienced some trouble in picking up his trail. Guided by a slight clue—he had been seen by some dock workers at Marseilles boarding a boat bound for the Black Sea—I followed him.

Across the wilds of Tartary and Russia, although he still evaded me, I followed his track. Sometimes peasants who had seen him informed me of his path. Sometimes he himself, who feared that if I lost all trace of him I should despair and die, left some mark to guide me. Cold, hunger and fatigue were the least pains which I was destined to endure. I was cursed by some devil and carried with me my eternal hell.

As I pursued my journey to the north, the snows thickened and the cold increased to a degree almost too severe to support. But I resolved not to fail in my purpose and, calling on Heaven to support me, I continued with unabated fervour to traverse immense deserts until the ocean appeared in the distance. Covered with ice, it could only be distinguished from land by its superior wildness and ruggedness. Some weeks before I had procured a sledge and dogs and travelled across the snows so rapidly that I was now but a day behind my quarry.

When I reached a tiny hamlet on the shore, I was told that a gigantic monster had put the inhabitants of a cottage to flight the night before and carried off their store of winter food. He had commandeered a dog sledge and set off across the frozen sea. I was desperate at the prospect which faced me: journeying across the mountainous ices amidst cold that few of the inhabitants could bear for long and which I, native of a temperate clime, could not hope to survive. Yet I knew I must go on to destroy that fiend and these stern emotions overwhelmed every other feeling.

Exchanging my land sledge for one more suited to ice travel and purchasing a plentiful stock of provisions, I departed. I judge that I passed three weeks on this journey and then, surmounting a ridge of ice, I saw, scarcely a mile distant, the monster on his sledge. My heart bounded within me but my hopes were suddenly extinguished as the sea swelled and, with the shock of an earthquake, the ice split. My enemy vanished and I was left marooned on a raft of ice. I was about to sink under the accumulation of distress when I saw your vessel, Captain Walton, and using part of the sledge as an oar was able to steer myself to your side.

CHAPTER FIVE

Robert Walton's Letters

To Mrs Saville, England
26th August 1788

YOU have read this strange and terrific story, Margaret, and no doubt feel your blood congeal with horror, as does mine. Sometimes, Frankenstein is seized by a sudden agony and cannot continue his tale. His fine and lovely eyes on occasions light up with indignation, and at other times are subdued to downcast sorrow. Sometimes he commands his countenance and tones and relates the most horrible incidents in a tranquil voice then, like a volcano bursting forth, his face suddenly changes to an expression of the wildest rage as he shrieks out imprecations on his persecutor.

A week has passed away while I have listened to his tale, the strangest that ever imagination formed. He is weak and I am afraid that I shall lose him. I have longed for a friend. I have sought one who would sympathise with and love me. Now, on these desert seas, I have found such a one but I fear I have gained him only to know his value and then see him die. I have tried to reconcile him to life, but he rejects the idea.

'I thank you, Walton,' he said yesterday, 'for your kind intentions but no new ties and fresh affections can replace those that are gone. Wherever I am, the soothing voice of my Elizabeth, and the conversation of Clerval, will ever be whispered in my ear. They are dead and but one feeling persuades me to preserve my life. I must pursue and destroy the being to whom I gave existence and then my work on earth will be fulfilled and I may die.'

Your affectionate brother, Robert Walton.

To Mrs Saville, England
12th September 1788

I write to you encompassed by peril, not knowing if I will ever see dear England again. I am surrounded by mountains of ice which threaten every moment to crush my vessel. The cold is excessive and already many of my unfortunate comrades have found a grave amidst this scene of desolation. Frankenstein daily declines in health, although a feverish fire still glimmers in his eye.

Seven days ago half a dozen sailors came to see me and their leader said that they had been chosen by the others to ask that, if the vessel be freed, I should direct my course southward. Although Frankenstein addressed them with some vigour, they refused to be swayed. I consented to return as soon as there is a way through the ice. I have lost my hopes of success and glory—and I have also lost my friend.

Three days past, the ice began to split and crack and was

driven with force towards the north; a breeze sprang up from the west and yesterday the passage towards the south became perfectly free. The sailors shouted with joy and Frankenstein awoke and asked the cause of the tumult.

'They shout,' I said, 'because they will soon return to England.'

'Go if you will,' he said, 'but I cannot. My purpose is assigned to me by Heaven and, although I am weak, the spirits who assist my vengeance will endow me with sufficient strength.'

Saying this, he tried to rise from his bed but the exertion was too great for him; he fell back, and fainted. When he awoke the surgeon gave him a composing draught but said that he had not long to live. I sat by his bed, watching him. Presently, he called me in a feeble voice, bidding me to come near.

'Alas! The strength I relied on is gone; I feel that I shall soon die, and my enemy and persecutor may still live. I have been occupied these last days in examining my past conduct and I find no fault therein. My duties towards my own species had the greatest claims to my attention and I did right by refusing to create a companion for the creature. He showed unparalleled malignity and selfishness. He destroyed my friends and I do not know where his thirst for vengeance may end. The task of his destruction was mine but I have failed. I ask you to undertake my unfinished work. Yet I cannot expect you to renounce your country and friends and, now that you are returning to England, you will have little chance of meeting with him. This hour, when I expect my release, is the only happy one which I have enjoyed for several years. Farewell, Walton! Seek happiness in peace and avoid ambition, even if it be only the apparently innocent one of distinguishing yourself in science and discoveries.'

His voice became fainter as he spoke and at length he sank into silence. Half an hour afterwards he attempted to speak but could not. He pressed my hand feebly and his eyes closed for ever.

I cannot express, my dear Margaret, the depth of sorrow which I feel. Tears flowed copiously at the untimely extinction of this glorious spirit. To relieve my grief, I stepped from the room of death into my own cabin for a while.

A little later, I heard the sound of a voice, human but hoarse, coming from the cabin where the remains of Frankenstein lay. I went in and over his lifeless body hung a form which I cannot find words to describe. Gigantic in stature, yet uncouth and distorted in its proportions. His face was concealed by long locks of ragged hair and one vast hand was extended, in colour and texture like that of a mummy. When he heard me he ceased uttering exclamations of grief and horror and sprang towards the window. Never before did I behold a vision of such loathsome hideousness as his face. I closed my eyes momentarily then, recollecting my duties towards this creature, I called on him to stay.

'That is also my victim!' he exclaimed. 'In his murder my crimes are consummated and the misery of my life is drawing to its close. Oh, Frankenstein! To no avail now I ask you to pardon me.'

The monster continued to utter wild and incoherent self-reproaches. I approached this tremendous being although I dare not raise my eyes to his face since there was something so scaring and unearthly in his ugliness.

'Your repentance,' I said, 'is superfluous. If you had heeded the stings of remorse, Frankenstein would yet have lived.'

'He did not suffer one ten-thousandth portion of the anguish that was mine. My heart was fashioned to hold out love and sympathy when, changed by misery to vice and hatred, it suffered such torture as even you cannot imagine. After the murder of Clerval, I returned to Switzerland, feeling pity for Frankenstein. But when I learnt that he was to be married, I recalled my threat and decided to carry it out. The completion of my demoniacal design became an insatiable passion. And now it is ended—there is my last victim!'

'It is not pity you feel,' I said. 'You lament only because the victim of your malignity is beyond your reach.'

'It is not so,' replied the creature. 'I am content to suffer alone. While I destroyed Frankenstein's hopes, I did not satisfy my own desires. I still wanted love and friendship and I was still spurned. Where was the justice in that? But it is true that I am a wretch. I have murdered the lovely and the helpless and driven my creator, one who is worthy of love and admiration, to his death. There he lies, white and cold; I have pursued him to that irredeemable ruin. But I will make no further mischief. My work is nearly complete. I shall quit your vessel on the ice-raft which brought me here and seek the northernmost point of the globe. I shall collect my funeral pyre and consume to ashes this miserable frame so that no man may discover how to create another such as I. Some years ago, when I felt the cheering warmth of summer and heard the rustling of the leaves and the warbling of the birds I should have wept to die. Now it is my only consolation. Farewell, Frankenstein! If you were yet alive and still desired revenge, it would be better satisfied in my continued life than in my destruction. I shall ascend my funeral pyre triumphantly and exult in the agony of the torturing flames. The light of the conflagration will fade and my ashes will be swept into the sea by the winds. My spirit will sleep in peace. Farewell!'

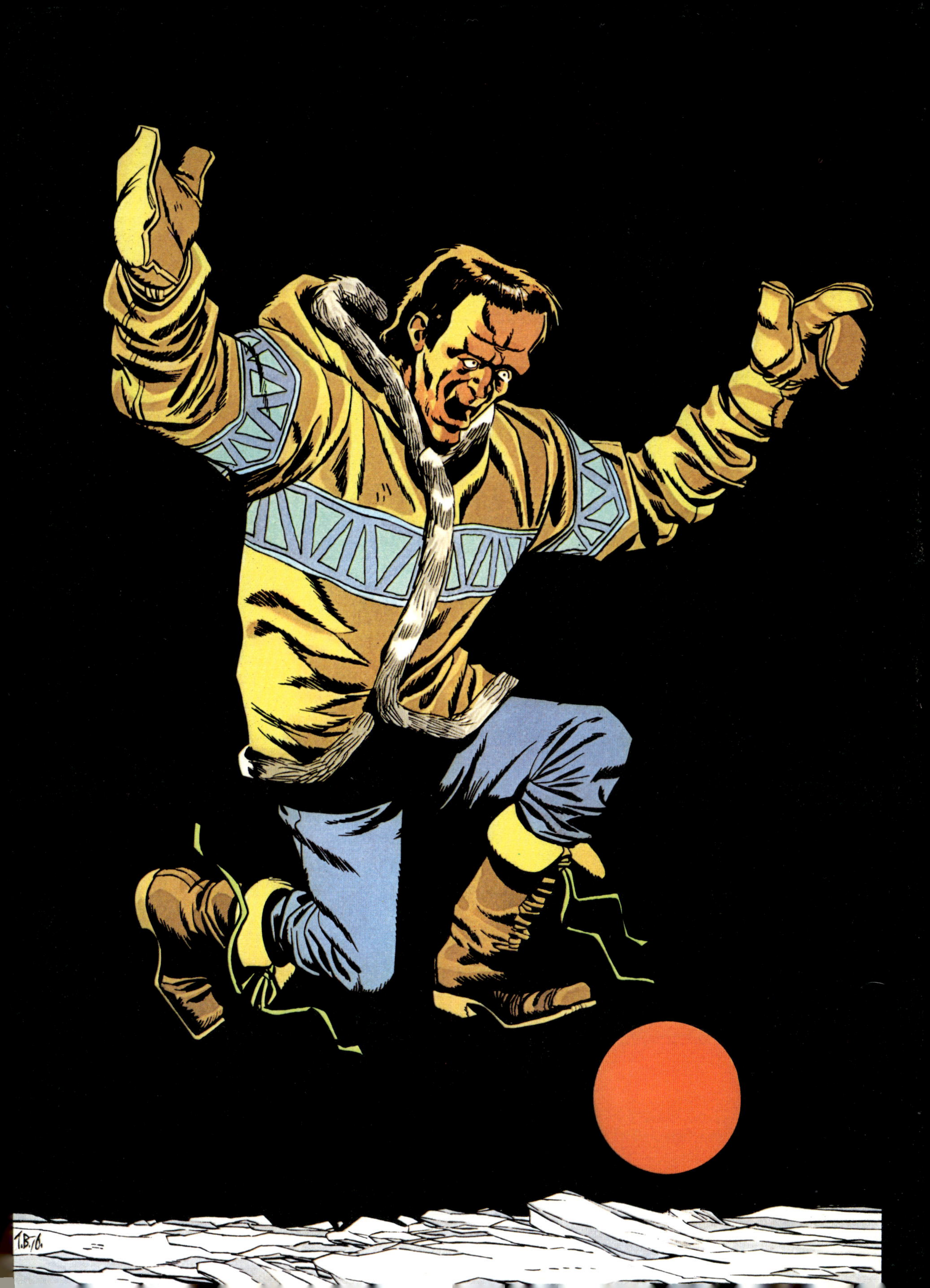

As he said this he sprang from the cabin window onto the ice-raft which lay close to the vessel. He was soon borne away by the waves and lost in darkness and distance.